ANYTHING CAN HAPPEN,
YOU JUST HAVE TO BELIEVE!

Minerva Mint

capstone
young readers

Minerva Mint is published by Capstone Young Readers
A Capstone Imprint
1710 Roe Crest Drive
North Mankato, Minnesota 56003
www.capstoneyoungreaders.com

© 2012 Atlantyca Dreamfarm s.r.l., Italy
© 2014 for this book in English language - Capstone Young Readers

Text by Elisa Puricelli Guerra; Translated by Chiara Pernigotti
Original edition published by Edizioni Piemme S.p.A., Italy
Original title: L'isola di Merlino

International Rights © Atlantyca S.p.A., via Leopardi 8 - 20123 Milano – Italia
foreignrights@atlantyca.it — www.atlantyca.com

Library of Congress Cataloging-in-Publication Data is available
on the Library of Congress website.

ISBN: 978-1-6237-0067-6 (hardcover)
ISBN: 978-1-4342-6511-1 (library binding)
ISBN: 978-1-4342-6514-2 (paperback)

Summary:
An overpowering archaeologist visits Pembrose to see Merlin's cave. Is it possible that this
is the famous sorcerer's cave or is it just a legend to attract tourists?

Designer:
Veronica Scott

Printed in China by Nordica.
1013/CA21301908
092013   007736NORDS14

MERLIN'S
ISLAND

by Elisa Puricelli Guerra
illustrated by Gabo León Bernstein

TABLE OF CONTENTS

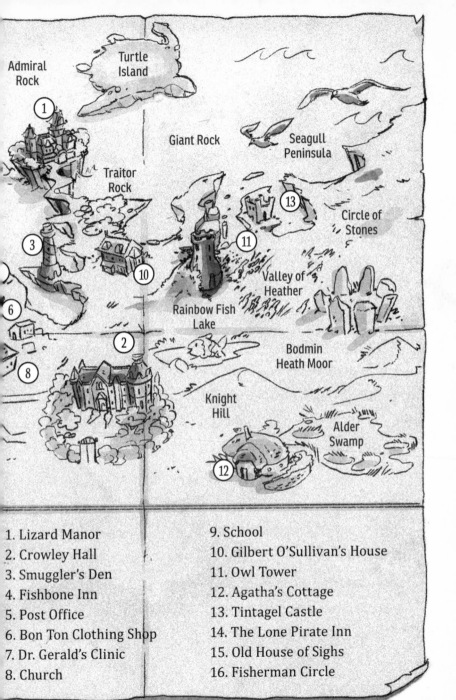

1. Lizard Manor
2. Crowley Hall
3. Smuggler's Den
4. Fishbone Inn
5. Post Office
6. Bon Ton Clothing Shop
7. Dr. Gerald's Clinic
8. Church
9. School
10. Gilbert O'Sullivan's House
11. Owl Tower
12. Agatha's Cottage
13. Tintagel Castle
14. The Lone Pirate Inn
15. Old House of Sighs
16. Fisherman Circle

WHAT'S HAPPENED SO FAR . . .

This is the story of Minerva Mint, a nine-year-old girl with fiery red hair. Minerva knows just one thing about her parents: they are incredibly forgetful. Well, at least she thinks they must be. They forgot her in a suitcase at Victoria Station in London when she was just a baby. Fortunately, an energetic custodian named Geraldine Flopps found her. Now Minerva and Mrs. Flopps live together at Lizard Manor, a run-down mansion that sits atop a cliff in Cornwall, England.

The suitcase in which Minerva was found was made of high-quality leather, with the initials MM carved on the brass lock. It was covered with labels from exotic places, suggesting it had traveled to Egypt, Beijing, Timbuktu, and Tahiti. In addition to baby Minerva, a number of other things were inside the bag: a thick book (Universal Encyclopedia, Vol. IV, M-P); *a letter with an odd message, addressed to a Mr. Septimus Hodge, Torrington Place, London; and the deed of property to Lizard Manor, which bore a lizard-shaped seal. Minerva believes these things are clues that could reveal her identity. For her entire life, she has been trying to unravel the mystery herself. But now, finally, she has some help: her new friends Ravi and Thomasina.*

Minerva has many questions she would like to answer. To start with, what happened to all the lizards at Lizard Manor? Why are there fourteen owls living on the roof? And will she ever find her parents?

Maybe it's Lizard Manor's magical qualities or her own mysterious origins, but Minerva's philosophy is that anything can happen, if you just believe. With that in mind she, together with Ravi and Thomasina, solved the mystery of the letter addressed to Septimus Hodge. They found a small box hidden in a kitchen wall at Lizard Manor. On the lid of the box was a drawing of a wide tower with two words carved in the wood: Ordo Noctuae: Order of the Owls. Inspired by the box, the three friends decided to found a club called the Order of the Owls to solve the mystery of Minerva's origins and help everyone in need. But first, they must find their own hideout ...

CHAPTER 1

SECRET MISSION

Minerva jumped all around her bedroom, wearing just one boot. She was already running late when she looked at herself in the mirror and realized that her dress was inside out and all the seams were showing.

"Shoot!" she said.

She undressed quickly, turned the dress right side out, and put it on correctly. Then she flew down the stairs at full speed.

Minerva found her other boot under the couch in living room number three, which Lizard Manor's family of foxes — Ginger, Cinnamon, and their beautiful, tawny-haired puppies — called home. One of the foxes must have gotten ahold of the boot and chewed up its edge, but Minerva wore it anyway. They were her lucky boots, and she needed luck that day. She was about to head out on an important expedition with her friends.

Minerva noticed that the window was open. It was spring outside; the sun was coming up and a slight fog hovered in the garden. A sweet, salty breeze blew in from the sea, and the grass was dotted with some little yellow and pink flowers that were still damp from the night.

A big white owl flew toward the roof saying, "*Woot! Woot!*"

"Hi, Augustus!" shouted Minerva, appearing at the window.

The owl kept flying upward, as solemn and quiet as a ghost. He joined the thirteen other owls that made their nest inside the house's crooked chimneys.

Minerva hurried to the hall, past the place where a big suit of armor missing an arm and leg stood, and threw open the door.

"Oh, no. I forgot something!" she said, turning around.

She flew back upstairs, ran into her bedroom, and pulled her beloved slingshot from underneath a pillow on the bed. Minerva admired it for a second — she had built it with her own hands and was very proud of it — then put it in her pocket. Now she was truly ready for adventure!

* * *

Outside, Minerva saw her guardian, Mrs. Flopps, pacing back and forth on the grass. She wore a Scottish cloak around

her shoulders and a soft hat on one side of her head. Under her arm, she carried an artist's easel, ready for her daily painting time. As she did every morning, Mrs. Flopps took deep breaths of the salty ocean air. This was how she prepared for her day.

"I'll see you around tea time!" shouted Minerva, running toward the gate. "I'm going to go look for a hideout with Ravi and Thomasina!"

Mrs. Flopps, still focusing all her efforts on her breathing, only said, "Um, okay, okay. Good."

Minerva ran breathlessly down a shortcut that led to the village. Luckily that day she didn't have to worry about being surprised by Gilbert's gang, who controlled the side of the cliff where she lived. Gilbert and his terrible dog, William the Conqueror, were in London, visiting an uncle.

Minerva celebrated her freedom with a series of cartwheels and then started running again. Her red locks danced in the wind as if they, too, were celebrating the beautiful day.

Lizard Manor, Minerva's home, sat atop Admiral

Rock, a cliff with an amazing view of the turquoise-green sea and Cornwall's coast. It was an ancient mansion with more than fifty rooms. The windows seemed to peer out at the world, and the whole house had a mysterious air surrounding it. People in town said that the mansion had been built by smugglers or pirates. After all, its position on top of the cliff was ideal for spotting the approaching English navy or a fleet of Spanish ships full of gold coins.

Minerva was supposed to meet Ravi and Thomasina at the Pembrose post office on Plum Tree Avenue, the town's main road. Plum Tree Avenue was also the site of the Fishbone Inn (the only place to stay in the village), one gray stone church, the Misses Bartholomew's fancy clothing shop, and Dr. Gerald's clinic.

The village was filled with excitement because the Sea Festival was coming up. The festival celebrated everything that was important in Cornwall: legends, food, music, and dancing. It was also the official start of Pembrose's tourist season, when camera-toting tourists invaded the sleepy, narrow, stone roads. Some of the tourists stayed in villagers' homes, while others lodged at the Fishbone Inn.

A tiny stream of green smoke floated out of the chimney at the Fishbone Inn. Timothy, the owner, was already awake. He was cooking his infamous pepper cod soup, which filled the air with a horrible smell.

Down by the port, on the small beach full of fishing nets, ropes, and lobster pots, fishermen prepared their stands for the fish market.

Ravi was already waiting outside the post office with his hands in his pockets. He looked anxious, and he kept trying to blow his long hair out of his eyes.

Minerva huffed and puffed as she finally arrived. She'd run all the way there, and now she could barely breathe. She bent over and tried to catch her breath. Once she felt better, she glanced up and noticed that there were three bicycles lying against the wall. She looked at her friend with a puzzled expression.

"These are for you and Thomasina," Ravi explained,

pointing at the two nicer bicycles. His was a piece of scrap metal with squeaky brakes. "I asked the school if I could borrow them — just for today. We'll be able to go farther on bikes than on foot."

"Wow!" Minerva's face, with all her freckles, lit up, and her big green eyes sparkled. She had never even sat on a bike before. Mrs. Flopps earned a living by selling paintings and homemade jams to tourists, but she barely made enough money to keep Lizard Manor going. There was never anything left over to buy something wonderful like a bicycle.

Ravi's mother appeared at the entrance of the post office. She held a big picnic basket that smelled delicious. "I made you all something for lunch!" she told Minerva, smiling.

"Oh, thank you, Mrs. Kapoor!"

Minerva really liked Ravi's mom. She thought she was beautiful. Mrs. Kapoor had long black hair that she wore loose on her shoulders. She had a tiny red bindi on her forehead, and she often wore beautiful saris from India. Best of all, Mrs. Kapoor was always happy and cheerful, despite the fact that she had to take care of the town's post office and grocery store all by herself.

Mrs. Kapoor tied the basket to Ravi's bike rack and reached out a hand to push Ravi's dark hair off his face, but she changed her mind and just said, "Have fun, darlings!"

With that, Mrs. Kapoor went back inside the store, jingling the curtain of bells that covered the doorway. Ravi mumbled a thank you, and his face relaxed. At his age, he could no longer stand his mom's hugs and kisses.

"Hey, you two!" a voice behind them said. "Don't you dare leave without me!"

Ravi and Minerva jumped. "Wow, Thomasina, you scared me to death!" the boy complained.

"That's not good. If you're part of a secret mission like this one, you have to be ready!" Thomasina scolded him.

She looked perfect, as usual, in a fluffy little summer dress. Her blond locks were tied back with a ribbon, and she was wearing a pair of shoes that looked quite uncomfortable. On her arm she carried her treasured purse. It held everything she might need during an adventure.

Adventure was, in fact, the magic word for the Order of the Owls — the secret club the three of them had founded to solve the mystery of Minerva's origins so she could find her parents.

However, in the last few months, they had been too busy to even work on that mystery. To outsiders, Pembrose might seem like the quietest fishing village in Cornwall. But there was always something that required the Order of the Owls' attention.

Before the three friends could focus on Minerva's parents, they had to find a secret hideout. They had been using Minerva's refuge — an abandoned lighthouse down the path from Admiral Rock. But evil Gilbert O'Sullivan's gang had found out about it, and the lighthouse was no longer safe. They had to find someplace new.

Thomasina pulled a map out of her purse and

pointed to the center of an area called Bodmin Heath Moor. The heath moor was a wild, nearly deserted place, with stretches of bare, rocky ridges and red heather plants. Going inside without a guide was definitely not recommended.

"I think this place would be perfect for our hide-out," said Thomasina. "Knight Hill."

Ravi leaned over to see where she was pointing. Of course, Knight Hill was miles away and completely isolated! He was certain they would get lost, but he didn't say a word. It didn't do any good to argue with Thomasina once she had decided something. She was used to giving orders to all the maids, butlers, and gardeners who served her family in the wonderful Crowley Hall. Plus she was really stubborn!

"I looked through some books last night," Thomasina said. She had access to many rare books in Crowley Hall's library. "The name of the hill comes from a boulder that sits on top. Supposedly, it's the rock that Excalibur was in."

"Really? Excalibur?" Minerva asked. "The sword

that was stuck in the stone until Arthur pulled it out?"

Everyone in that area knew the legends of King Arthur, the Knights of the Round Table, and Merlin the sorcerer. After all, King Arthur had been born near Pembrose. His birthplace, Tintagel Castle, was a favorite tourist destination.

"Well, the truth is people don't know if that's the rock for sure . . ." Thomasina admitted. "But it could be!"

"Sure, it could!" echoed Minerva. Like her friend, she believed that anything was possible.

"The most important thing," Thomasina added, "is that there's an old fortress on the hill. It's off the main path, so it's perfect for our secret hideout. What do you think?"

"Wow!" said Minerva. "I'm so excited!"

"Well," mumbled Ravi, "if we can get there . . ."

"What did you say?" asked Thomasina.

"Nothing," answered Ravi. He definitely didn't want to start his day by arguing with his friend.

Ravi and Thomasina had been friends since his first day of school in Pembrose. He still remembered the teacher sitting him next to the beautiful Thomasina Crowley. He'd immediately fallen in love with her. She even made him forget that he was homesick for India. Too bad that every time Thomasina opened her mouth, he disagreed with her and they ended up fighting!

Ravi pointed at the bicycle. He knew that Thomasina's parents didn't want her to ride a bike because they didn't think it was ladylike. So he figured his surprise would make her happy.

Thomasina, in fact, was immediately thrilled. She put the map back in her purse and easily hopped on the bike. "Well, what are you two waiting for? Follow me!" she shouted, pedaling away.

Minerva slowly climbed on her bike. It was her first time on a bicycle, and she felt a little unsure and unsteady. She put her feet on the pedals, but both she and the bike immediately tumbled to the ground.

Ravi helped her get up, and then he hopped on his

own bike. "It's not difficult," he said, encouraging her. "Do what I do."

"I don't need any help!" insisted Minerva. She had learned to do a lot of things by herself. She had learned to climb trees like a squirrel and swim like a fish. She could even drive a boat. She wasn't going to stop learning on her own because of a bike! She put her feet on the pedals once again and started. She was shaky, but at least she didn't fall this time. She kept pedaling, unsteadily at first. But soon she felt sure of herself — so sure, in fact, that in moments she was riding like her friends, swerving in and out of the narrow streets of the village.

Riding a bicycle was amazing. Minerva loved how the wind felt on her face and how her hair flew around like crazy.

"Hurray, I passed you!" she yelled as soared past Ravi and Thomasina on the path overlooking the turquoise sea.

The path was so narrow that she almost ran over a young hiker carrying a backpack. He was handsome with long blond hair and green eyes. He jumped to the side to get out of Minerva's way, but he didn't look angry. Instead, he gave them a big smile as they biked past.

"I wonder who he is," said Thomasina with a sigh. She kept looking behind her. "He's so cute, and he seems sort of noble in a way. That's how I imagine the great knights of King Arthur's round table looked . . ."

"Hey, watch where you're going!" yelled Ravi, feeling a flash of jealousy. He turned and glared back at his rival but ended up crashing into a thorny bush. "Ouch!" he yelled. "Hey, wait for me!"

CHAPTER 2

THE HEATH MOOR

Minerva and her friends spent the morning exploring Bodmin Heath Moor. Across the rocky fields, they found a herd of wild ponies running free and a small blue lake filled with red fish. They also found the ruins of an old lodge. It was probably once a hiding place for smugglers.

But as hard as they looked, they could not find Knight Hill. Thomasina led them to the top of every hill she could find. But none were the right one. The old fortress was nowhere to be found.

"I can't take it anymore!" said Ravi. He fell on the

grass together with his bike. He was worn out, all of his muscles hurt, and he was starving. He hoped the lunch his mom had packed was huge. "We're clearly on the wrong road!"

"Oh, really?" said Thomasina, stomping up to him. "And what makes you think that?"

"The fact that we can't find what we're looking for," said Ravi with his eyes closed.

"But the map . . ." said Thomasina, kneeling at his side. "Look!" She took the map out of her purse and pointed at their destination.

Ravi opened his eyes and lifted his head a bit. Then he let it fall with a groan. "Ugh! You're holding it upside down. We went the exact opposite way!"

"Really? Well, why didn't you say so sooner?" asked Thomasina, annoyed.

"I say we eat," Minerva interrupted. She wanted to change the subject, and she knew it was important to eat. It was always hard to think on an empty stomach, and there was a good chance that you would end up arguing when you felt hungry.

They spread out a checkered tablecloth and

unpacked their delicious picnic. There were big ham and cheese sandwiches, orange sodas, crisp Cornish pasties, and big slices of blueberry and cinnamon cream pie. The three friends ate happily.

Full and satisfied, they lay on the grass and gazed up at the clouds drifting in the sky.

"I'm never moving from this spot," said Ravi, sighing.

"But we haven't found the hideout yet!" protested Minerva. She was ready to go again.

"We don't even know if it exists!" said Ravi.

"Well, we have to try!" Minerva insisted. "It'll be a place of our own."

"A secret place. A special, secret place!" added Thomasina. "We'll use it as a base for our missions. The first will be to find Minerva's parents. We've already found the flute."

Minerva automatically touched the small flute hanging on a chain around her neck. They had found it in a secret opening in a kitchen wall at Lizard Manor, thanks to the instructions in a letter. The letter was one of several clues Minerva had about her identity. When she was just a baby, the girl and clues were left together inside a suitcase at a train station.

The three friends had also discovered that the sound of the flute seemed to attract owls. Whenever Minerva played it, a parliament of owls appeared — so many that they made the sky turn black!

Why was the flute hidden? Was it my parents' flute? Minerva thought about her parents more and more now that her friends were helping her try to find them. *Why did they leave me at Victoria Station? Did they forget about me? Or did something happen to them?*

Her thoughts were interrupted by an excited bark. Minerva, Thomasina, and Ravi barely had time to sit up before a black dog jumped on their laps. He was a big dog, like a cross between a lab and some sort of setter. A clump of dark fur covered his eyes.

"Ouch!" yelled Ravi. He had eaten like a pig, and his belly ached right where the dog had leaped.

"Who are you?" asked Thomasina, petting the dog.

The dog barked happily.

"Pendragon! Pendragon, come here!" someone called.

The kids glanced up and saw a young woman running toward them. She tried to grab the dog, who was furiously licking the faces of all three children, one after the other.

"Pendragon, behave! Come on!" the young woman

ordered, looking embarrassed. "I'm so sorry. He doesn't look like it, but he's still a puppy."

"Oh, don't worry," said Minerva. "He's so cute!" She sank her face into the dog's soft fur, while Thomasina scratched his belly.

The young woman tried to pull the dog away again, but with no luck. Pendragon had found some wonderful new friends.

"Would you like a slice of pie?" Ravi asked, brushing dog hair from his shirt. "My mom made it."

The young woman smiled. She had a unique face and long black hair that touched her waist. Her skin was as white as milk, and her wide, blue eyes sparkled like crystal lakes.

"Sure, thanks." She sighed and looked at Pendragon with one eyebrow raised. The dog was happily tackling his new friends. Ravi handed her a slice of pie and then fed one to the dog, who thoroughly enjoyed it.

The young woman introduced herself with a shy smile. "I'm Agatha Willow, by the way."

Ravi, Minerva, and Thomasina were shocked. They knew all about Agatha Willow! The townspeople said she was a witch or a healer. She lived by herself in a cottage in the heath moor, and she was known for making wild plants into medicine. She rarely went to the village, and when she did, she visited the Bartholomew sisters, her only friends. They ran a small clothing shop that doubled as a tourist office during the summer.

Minerva could not hold her tongue. "Oh, then you know everything about the heath moor!" she shouted.

Agatha smiled slightly. "I see you've heard about me."

Minerva blushed. "Well, Gwendolyn Bartholomew says that when she needs to learn something about the history of the heath moor and places to visit, she asks you."

Agatha bit into her pie. "That's true. I give her suggestions for tourists who want to visit the heath moor."

"Then you must know where Knight Hill is!" said Thomasina. She was petting Pendragon's head, which rested on her legs.

Agatha chewed slowly. "Yes. Why are you interested? It's very far from here and there's nothing to see, except for a few boulders."

Thomasina's face fell. "Oh, we were looking for a place for our hideout. I thought there was a fortress up on the hill and the stone . . ."

". . . that Excalibur was stuck in," Agatha finished the sentence. "Well, there's nothing left of the fortress, but there are plenty of boulders. Who knows? Maybe one of them really is Excalibur's stone." She winked at them.

"So, do you believe in the story of Excalibur?" asked Thomasina, excited once again.

"Sure. I believe in all sorts of things. There's much more in this world than what we see. You just have to learn how to look for it."

"Do you believe in Merlin, too?" Minerva asked. "Did he really exist?"

Agatha nodded with a serious expression on her face. Her eyebrows narrowed. "Merlin was the son of a very powerful fairy and a human. His father was a handsome prince who seduced the fairy," she started.

Ravi was filled with doubt. He thought that she was messing with them, but she was nice to listen to anyway. Her voice was almost musical, and it was impossible not to stare at her blue eyes. Thomasina and Minerva were hanging on her every word.

"But a union between a human and a fairy is not allowed, so Merlin's birth was not blessed," Agatha continued. "The night when he was born, everyone saw doomful signs in the sky. Lightning ripped through the darkness. A furious wind blew on every single thing. The moon became red . . ."

Pendragon howled to emphasize how dramatic that night was. His howl interrupted Agatha's thoughts, and she looked at the sun and said, "Oh, it's getting late. Someone's waiting for me in Caldebury. I'm sorry, but I've got to go!" She got up and grabbed Pendragon by his collar.

"No, please stay!" begged Thomasina.

"Tell us more!" added Minerva.

Agatha smiled apologetically. "Come see me one of these days. My house is near Alder Swamp. Interesting herbs grow close to water, you know." She yanked Pendragon. "Let's go, little piggy!"

The dog sadly parted from his new friends.

"Thanks for the pie!" shouted Agatha, walking away.

The three friends were finally rested. They looked at each other, unsure of what to do now that their idea for the perfect hideout was out.

"Well, since it's pointless to go to Knight Hill now, how about a swim in that beautiful lake with the red fish?" suggested Minerva. After the long bike ride, a dip sounded like the perfect way to cool off.

"But the water is going to be freezing!" complained Ravi.

"Even better. Let's see who can jump in first!" Minerva shouted, running to get her bike.

Thomasina, of course, was up for the challenge and immediately jumped on her bike.

Ravi sighed. "Well, I don't have permission to swim after lunch!"

* * *

When Minerva returned to Lizard Manor that afternoon, Mrs. Flopps was sipping tea in the yard. A plate of delicious, warm scones sat on the table next to her, along with a jar of thick cream and some of her homemade strawberry jam.

Dried mud spattered Minerva's face full of freckles. She had a bruise on her knee, and her dress was dirty, wet, and torn from falling off her bike.

But Mrs. Flopps didn't even notice how she looked. "A cup of tea?" she asked. "The scones are straight from the oven."

Minerva sank into a wicker chair and happily bit into a scone. It was still warm and crispy.

She started telling Mrs. Flopps about everything that had happened on that wonderful day.

Meanwhile, the old woman was inspired by the afternoon light. She took a notebook in her hands and started to sketch the cliffs' jagged profile.

* * *

That evening, Minerva, her friends, and all the villagers gathered down at Pembrose's port. At eight o'clock, the Happy Fisherman's choir started to sing old sea ballads underneath a big tent. The 100th Annual Pembrose Sea Festival had officially begun. The retired Colonel Marmaduke Gunfire-Artillery then gave a boring speech. He thanked everyone who contributed to the event, especially the Pembrose Ladies Committee.

Locals and tourists walked around the stalls, which sold handcrafted products and fish delicacies. Very few people, though, got close to Timothy's stall. The owner of the only lodge in the village was a terrible cook. His soups and fish mixtures caused painful stomachaches, but no one had the courage to tell him.

The only person who dared to buy a bag of fried fish was Gwendolyn Bartholomew. She looked lovely in a dress that was identical to her sister Araminta's. Her long blond hair was piled up on top of her head, making her look even taller than her height of nearly six feet! She sent Timothy dreamy looks through the round lenses of her glasses. Everyone knew she was in love with him. Everyone except Timothy.

Minerva, Ravi, and Thomasina sat on the pier, sharing some candy and listening to the fisherman's choir. The sun was just setting, and purple and pink stripes floated on the water. The wind always blew in that part of Cornwall, but that evening it was particularly strong, lifting skirts and messing hair.

Minerva gazed at the scene, feeling content. Looking over the crowd, she spotted the handsome young man she had almost hit on her bike. He was walking through the crowd, his green eyes scanning faces like he was searching for someone.

Minerva nudged Thomasina. "There's the guy from this morning," she whispered.

"Where?" her friend asked. She looked around, but the stranger was already gone.

"I wonder who he is," said Thomasina, sighing.

Ravi immediately became jealous. "Shhh! If you keep talking I won't be able to hear the choir!" he said.

After a few minutes, Thomasina grabbed a candy and whispered, "Hey guys, there's something I have to tell you. Mom and Dad are planning a fox hunt tomorrow —"

"Oh, no!" interrupted Minerva. She loved all animals. She couldn't stand the thought of someone hunting a defenseless fox.

"A lot of guests will be there," continued Thomasina. "Horrible people from London . . ."

Minerva squeezed her fists. Her face grew red with anger. "We have to sabotage the hunt!" she declared.

"You're right!" agreed Thomasina. "Do you have an idea?"

"Of course!" said Minerva with a twinkle in her eyes.

Ravi felt a shiver go down his spine. He knew nothing good could come from this.

Sensing his hesitation, Minerva gave him a pat on the back. "Come on, Ravi. It'll be fun!"

Ravi just rolled his eyes. Minerva would drag them into trouble once again!

Suddenly, a strong gust of wind tore through the port, ripping up the Happy Fisherman's tent. It flew over the audience and landed on the stage where the festival's honored guests sat. Colonel Gunfire-Artillery was buried in the colorful fabric. Everyone hurried to save him, and the evening came to an abrupt end.

On the way home, the people of Pembrose mumbled to each other. Everyone agreed that what had happened was not a good sign. Some type of misfortune was definitely coming their way.

CHAPTER 3

FOX HUNT

The next day, Minerva was looking for something elegant to wear to Thomasina's house. Her friend's house was practically a castle, and her parents liked things to be perfect. Everything in Crowley Hall was flawless, from the evenly trimmed grass, to the delicacies of the French cook, to the formal manners of everyone who lived there.

Minerva stuck her head in a big chest. She remembered seeing some old-fashioned dresses in there. They would be perfect for a visit to Thomasina's.

Suddenly, Minerva heard a terrible noise. Fortunately, the house was not falling down — an event that both she and Mrs. Flopps figured would happen sooner or later. Rather, it was the sound of Ravi's bike brakes.

"Minerva!" Ravi shouted up from the yard. "Minerva!"

Minerva's head popped out of the chest, and she hurried to the front door, trampling her long dress along the way. A long pearl necklace dangled around her neck, and she wore a feathered hat that could hardly find its balance on her wild locks of hair.

Ravi was delivering a package that had come to the post office for Minerva. Then they planned to look for some clothing for him. There was no way he could show up to an event at Sir Archibald and Lady Annabella's castle in his usual old pair of jeans.

When Minerva opened the door, Ravi was staring nervously at a stone lizard that sat on the edge of a fishpond by the entrance. Minerva had told him over and over that there were no lizards in her house, but he didn't believe her. If there were no lizards, then why was the place called Lizard Manor? Ravi was victim of many phobias, including a fear of heights, but the fear of lizards was his biggest one. He was horrified by the way they darted around so quickly. And he hated their detaching tails and ugly heads. He thought they looked like prehistoric dragons.

But when he saw Minerva wearing a terrible ruffled and lacey dress, he forgot about his fears. "What are you wearing?" he asked with his eyes wide.

Minerva dragged him inside without answering him. "Come on in!" she said. "Or we're going to be late!"

They left the package in kitchen number three (number one was flooded and number two was all smoky because of a malfunctioning stove), and they went upstairs.

Ravi followed Minerva, trying not to step on her dress while he looked at the portraits of her ancestors hanging on the walls. Those little narrow eyes, severe noses, and arched eyebrows gave him shivers. The ancestors looked like they disapproved of him.

They entered Minerva's room. A yellow tent stood in the middle of the room. This is where the girl slept. Her high bed, with the brass headboard, was very uncomfortable. And because the roof was full of holes, she always faced the risk of getting rained on in her bedroom. Sleeping inside a tent seemed like the most practical and fun solution!

On the nightstand, there was the small box that the Order of the Owls had found a couple of months earlier. It was the box that held Minerva's little flute. A round, stone tower was carved into the lid, along with the words *Ordo Noctuae* — Latin for *Order of the Owls.*

"So, how do I look?" asked Minerva, spinning.

Ravi stepped back to leave room for her wide skirt that opened like a bell when she spun. "Very good!" he answered automatically. He had learned from his mother to use careful manners with women.

Minerva stopped twirling suddenly and started

giggling as she jumped on one foot and then the other.

"Excuse me," said Ravi right away. "You don't look very good. You look crazy!"

Minerva immediately stopped hopping around. Like many things about her, the secret of her ticklish feet was kind of hard to explain. Whenever someone lied to her, she felt a tingle on her toes and started giggling. And giggling. And giggling! That's how she knew whether someone was telling the truth or not.

Still shaking with laughter, Minerva said, "Really? Well, actually I didn't even think it looked good. Come on, let's look in here." She opened a big closet.

Minerva had never bought a single dress or pair of shoes. She found everything she needed in the closets and old chests of the thirty-one bedrooms at Lizard Manor. The house held clothes of every size and for all ages. All of these old clothes had been put away with extreme care. They were hung carefully or wrapped up in layers of tissue paper so that they would not get ruined.

The two friends tried on many items. Finally, they decided on a charming taffeta dress with a high waist and ruffles for Minerva and a wonderful Indian suit with embroidered shoes and a red turban for Ravi.

"Maybe this suit belonged to an ancestor who visited India," Minerva suggested. She looked at her friend with a critical eye and added, "It looks great on you! You really look like a *maharaja*."

By then, they were running late, so they both jumped on Ravi's bike. (They had already returned Minerva's, and she missed it terribly.) Minerva carried a bag with her, but when Ravi asked what was in it, all she would say was, "A surprise."

As they left the house in a hurry, fourteen pairs of eyes watched them. The owls studied everything from Lizard Manor's rooftop.

* * *

When Ravi and Minerva arrived at Crowley Hall, a distinguished butler stood at the entrance. "Could I ask for your names?" he asked suspiciously.

Minerva lifted her chin a bit. "Minerva Mint from Lizard Manor!" she announced.

"And Maharaja from Bombay," said Ravi in a solemn tone.

The butler didn't look convinced, but fortunately, Thomasina got there just in time. "Ravi, you look great!" she exclaimed.

The boy blushed. "Um, thank —" he started.

"Come on," said Thomasina without letting him finish. She brought them to the yard where the guests, all dressed up for the hunt, were stuffing themselves with salmon canapés.

"Wait here," Thomasina whispered secretively. "I have to check on something." She left her friends and disappeared into the back of the house.

Minerva and Ravi looked around curiously. Up until that point, Ravi had thought it had been fun dressing up like a maharaja and getting compliments from Thomasina . . . but now he was worried. What did his friend have in mind?

Minerva distracted him by pointing off to their right. "That must be the terrible gardener Thomasina keeps talking about," she whispered. Their friend often argued with Crowley Hall's chief gardener, Angus McAllister, because he accused her of walking on the grass that he tended lovingly. The cranky gardener was guarding the flowerbeds. His eyes, surrounded by thick red eyebrows, seemed to threaten, *Just try to step on my flowers. See what happens.*

"Let's walk around a bit," whispered Ravi as he eyed a tray with some delicious-looking treats on it.

Just then, the sound of a horn echoed, and the hunters started to go toward the stables.

Ravi had just managed to grab one of the delicious treats when Thomasina reappeared.

"*Psst*, come here!" she whispered, dragging her friends with her. "Time for Minerva's plan."

Oh, no! thought Ravi, choking on a bite of his fancy food.

Minerva and Thomasina's plans always ended up in complete disaster. Like that time when he found himself hanging from Traitor Rock, nearly falling into the valley twenty-some feet under him.

The three friends hid behind a pile of hay bales close to the stables. All the hunters were almost ready to go, and the dogs were impatient and ready to follow the fox's tracks. Sir Archibald and Lady Annabella were exchanging the last instructions.

Minerva gave the bag to Thomasina. "Here's what we need," she said.

Thomasina grabbed the bag, reached inside, and pulled out a pillow.

"It's from one of the couches where Ginger and Cinnamon sleep at Lizard Manor," explained Minerva.

"Perfect," said Thomasina. "I'm sure it'll work."

Ravi looked at one girl, then the other. "Hey, what do you two have in mind?"

Minerva smiled apologetically. "I'm sorry, Ravi, we didn't tell you anything because we knew you'd complain."

Ravi crossed his arms, offended. "Oh, really?"

"Minerva's plan is perfect," said Thomasina. "The dogs will follow this pillow's scent, thinking it's the fox."

"They'll leave the real fox alone, and it'll have plenty of time to get far away from here, since the hunters will be . . ." continued Minerva.

"They'll be following you," concluded Thomasina.

"Me?" said Ravi, shaking.

Thomasina gave him the pillow. "Take this and run down there," she ordered, pointing out a path. "If you go behind the stables, no one will see you. Head out from the small gate and go straight ahead through the woods. There's a muddy lake down there. That's where you should hide. The water will confuse the dogs. They'll go in circles, and the horses will get stuck in the mud . . ."

Ravi was listening, but he could not say a word.

"Are you following me?" asked Thomasina, surprised by his silence.

Ravi shook himself. "I don't . . ."

Right then the horn sounded again.

"Hurry, we don't have much time!" said Thomasina. She put the pillow in Ravi's hands and kissed him on the cheek. "Go, my hero!" she said.

Ravi started to run. What else was he supposed to do after his crush called him her hero? He ran behind the stables with the pillow in his hands and kept going toward the woods. He barely made it inside the thick of the trees before the horn sounded for the third time and the horses left at full gallop behind the dogs.

At first, everything seemed fine. Thomasina pulled a pair of binoculars from her precious purse. She took a look and then passed them to Minerva.

Sir Archibald and Lady Annabella rode fiercely at the head of the group. Soon though, Minerva noticed that something was wrong. The riders looked very stiff. Some tried to stop their horses. But the dogs, excited by the smell of the fox, continued their chase. The horses didn't want to stop when they were so close to the fox either. So, even if the riders yelled and pulled the reigns, the hunt went on.

"I don't get it," said Minerva, looking at everything with the binoculars. "Everyone looks angry . . ."

Thomasina grinned. "I wasn't sure the pillow plan would work, so I prepared another surprise," she explained. "I put glue on the saddles."

Minerva gasped. Her friend was really devilish!

"The hunters won't be able to get off before they get to the lake," continued Thomasina. "It'll take a long time to un-glue themselves from the saddles."

"Take that!" said Minerva. "In the future, they'll think twice before hunting, especially here at Crowley Hall!"

Thomasina giggled. "Yes, take that!" she said with satisfaction.

"Help!" one of the far-off hunters yelled before disappearing into the woods with the others.

"Plan complete!" said Thomasina, putting the

binoculars away. "Want to go eat some finger sand-wiches?" she suggested to Minerva. "There's also Madame Cosette's chocolate cake. It's so delicious. Too bad Ravi is going to miss it."

"Well, we could save a slice for him," said Minerva generously.

CHAPTER 4

THE BEAUTIFUL STRANGER

The next day at school, Ravi refused to speak to Thomasina. He didn't even look at her once. He ignored her blue eyes and blond hair, her excuses and sweet-talking. He was just too upset!

The previous afternoon, he'd managed to get away and back to his friends without the hunters seeing him. But nothing — not even the chocolate cake they offered him — made him feel better. It was going to take him a while to forgive them.

Only on the way home from school, when

Thomasina climbed on his bike behind him and put her arms around his waist, did Ravi start to calm down.

By the time they reached the center of Pembrose, Ravi had forgotten all about his anger. He was distracted by everything that was going on in town. Everyone was talking about two things. First of all, they gossiped about the Crowley's terrible hunt. It was a complete disaster. The guests left offended, and Madame Cosette, who had prepared lunch for thirty people who didn't even touch her food, was threatening to quit.

The second topic was definitely more interesting: a mysterious stranger had come to town! He wasn't a tourist. (It was easy to spot tourists, because they wore big cameras and were always checking a map.) He wasn't one of Sir Archibald and Lady Annabella's snobbish guests, either. So who was he?

When Ravi and Thomasina got to the post office, Orazia Haddok, Dr. Gerald's gossipy nurse, was standing at the entrance talking with Ravi's mom.

"I bet he's from London," the nurse said, scrunching her nose. "Remember my words, Mrs. Kapoor, nothing good comes from London!"

Just then, a handsome man with long blond hair exited the Bartholomew sisters' store.

"That's him!" whispered Thomasina.

"Yes, he's the man we met in the heath moor," mumbled Ravi with an upset look.

Ms. Haddok wrinkled her nose again, like she smelled something terrible. Then she walked away, swinging her grocery bags.

Ravi's mom shook her head as if to clear it of the nurse's words and smiled at the children. "How was school today? Do you two want a snack?"

But they weren't listening. They were eyeing the stranger, who was headed up the path out of town, whistling.

"What do you think he's doing here?" whispered Thomasina.

"And why is he walking around the cliffs?" whispered Ravi.

Mrs. Kapoor gave up and sighed. "If you get hungry, there's some banana pie," she said, going back inside the store.

Ravi and Thomasina looked at each other.

"The only way to find out about him is to ask the Bartholomew sisters," said Ravi.

"Exactly what I was thinking!" agreed Thomasina.

"I only hope they don't start talking . . ." said Ravi. The Bartholomew sisters were known for being especially chatty.

The Bartholomew sisters' store was called Bon Ton. In their small space, they crammed mannequins, little couches, mirrors, hats, and clothes.

Gwendolyn, who was nearly six feet tall, always ran the risk of bumping her head on the low ceiling. On the other hand, the short and chubby Araminta did not run that risk. The two sisters followed a rather old-fashioned style in their collections: long dresses with narrow waists, high collars, and puffy sleeves. And they always wore matching dresses in that style.

When Ravi and Thomasina entered the store, the

sisters were busy putting away some teacups.

"Oh, dear!" said Araminta. "What a pleasure! Would you like a cookie? I think I have some left —"

"Araminta," her sister interrupted, "maybe Thomasina came to get a dress made."

Araminta put down the cup she was holding in her hands. "Oh, dear," she said, hurrying to get some fabric samples. "Let me show you some samples."

Thomasina stopped her. "No! I mean, maybe another time. We . . . well . . . we were curious about that man who just left the store."

Araminta's eyes sparkled. "Oh, dear, such a hand-some young man!"

"He's an archaeologist," explained Gwendolyn.

"A *very famous* archaeologist," added Araminta. "He just came from London."

"His name is Tristam Awsome," Gwendolyn went on. "He graduated with three degrees from Oxford and now works at the British Museum."

"Why was he in your store?" asked Ravi.

"He wanted some information on the village.

We're also a tourist office during this busy season, you know," said Araminta, pointing to the sign hanging on the door. It read *Bon Ton: Fashion and Tourism.*

"He's camping close to Tintagel. He's down there studying the ruins of Arthur's castle and Merlin's cave . . . the one you can only access during low tide," said Gwendolyn. "He said he's about to make a very important discovery."

Ravi and Thomasina looked at each other.

"Merlin again!" Thomasina whispered.

"And didn't he say anything else?" asked Ravi.

"No, but he plans to make an announcement soon," answered Gwendolyn.

Araminta sighed. "So young and he's already an archaeology expert."

Ravi and Thomasina quickly said goodbye and left the store, declining a cup of tea.

"We have to tell Minerva everything!" said Thomasina. "I'm just not sure about that Tristam. He's too perfect. This could be a mystery for the

Order of the Owls!"

Ravi, happy that "that Tristam" was not only an object of admiration but also scrutiny, said, "Hop on!"

And off they went to Lizard Manor.

* * *

Minerva was studying in the library. Or really, she was *pretending* to study in the library. The truth was she was experimenting with a new method of balancing three big volumes — very boring ones — on her head while standing on one foot.

Minerva did not attend the local school. Instead, she was "privately instructed," as she put it. Since she was very curious, she read and conducted experimental lessons on just about every topic all by herself. That day, for example, she had decided to study ancient Rome. She wore a tunic and a hat with feathers for a helmet. The volumes she balanced on her head were all about Roman history.

When she heard the horrible squeaking of Ravi's bicycle, Minerva let the books fall. She was happy to have something much more interesting to do than study. She hurried to the entrance, but was stopped by Hugo the badger, who fell at her feet. As usual, he had suddenly popped out from one of the tunnels he had dug under the house.

When Ravi and Thomasina walked into the house, along with Mrs. Flopps, they found their friend on the floor and Hugo lying by her side with a feathered hat on his head.

* * *

The Order of the Owls talked about Tristam Awsome all afternoon. Mrs. Flopps took care of the snacks: warm scones and strawberry jam. It was the perfect food to stimulate the brain and increase focus while working to uncover beautiful strangers' mysterious plots.

"Why would a famous archaeologist wander into our town?"

"What's the announcement he wants to make?"

"We need to keep an eye on him!" the three

decided unanimously. With that taken care of, they dedicated their undivided attention to the scones.

For the next several days, the Order spied on all the famous archaeologist's moves. Tristam spent most of his days at Tintagel Castle. They watched him with Thomasina's binoculars: he gathered rock samples and used a series of stills, small stoves, and powders for his analysis. When it was low tide, he went down to Merlin's cave. For this work, he usually wore some weird, transparent glasses that covered half of his face, and he always came back with several samples to analyze.

He showed up in town more and more often. He visited the Bartholomew sisters and questioned the oldest residents. It seemed like he had a good relationship with Timothy.

And half of Pembrose's females were in love with him! Girls hoping to get married competed to get him to share a cup of tea with them. They would appear all dressed up, wearing fancy hats made by the Bartholomew sisters. Tristam seemed to enjoy all of the attention. His blond hair was always a perfect mess, and his smile was mesmerizing.

One day, the three friends were following him to Tintagel. They were certain he didn't know they were there, but he suddenly turned sharply.

"Aha! I knew you were there!" he exclaimed.

Caught off guard, Ravi, Minerva, and Thomasina stopped abruptly in the middle of the trail.

Tristam wore one of his sparkling smiles that had conquered many girls' hearts in Pembrose. "Why are you following me, you three?"

"Well, um . . . we're very interested in archaeology," said Ravi.

Tristam raised one eyebrow. "Really?"

Ravi threw a worried look toward Minerva, who was trying not to laugh. "Well, not really," he admitted.

Minerva decided to tell the truth. "We wanted to find out why you're here, and why you're so interested in Tintagel."

"You're curious, huh?"

"Yes," said Thomasina. "And we're interested in Merlin the sorcerer."

Tristam ran his hand through his hair to put it back in place as if the wind had messed it up. "I'm very interested in him, too," he started.

Minerva nudged Ravi and smirked. "I think he's more interested in his own hair," she whispered.

"What did you say?" asked Tristam, raising an eyebrow.

"Oh, nothing. I just wondered why you're interested in Merlin."

Tristam put his hand back into his hair again, not noticing Ravi's and Minerva's giggles. "Well, I'm an archaeologist, and I specialize in the Middle Ages," he started in a wise tone. "People say that Arthur was born inside Tintagel Castle . . . and it could be true. There's an inscription with his name that might prove it. But is it true that Merlin practiced his magic in the cave underneath the castle? And that he helped Arthur become King? Or is it just a legend?"

"What do you mean . . . a legend?" asked Minerva.

"A fairytale, for those who want to believe in magic," said Tristam, spreading his arms. "I believe in science. I'm sorry to disappoint you, but I did several inspections and . . . well, it seems that Merlin has never been inside that cave."

The three friends looked at him, their mouths open in shock. A spark of anger flashed in Minerva's eyes. She wanted to tell him about Agatha and all she had told them in the heath moor.

But Tristam wouldn't let her. "I would love to believe that the fairytales are true," he continued. "But I'm determined to find out the truth once and for all. I'm waiting for my team of experts from London to carry out a final inspection. I'm sure they'll agree with me — Merlin's cave is a fake."

Minerva was ready to argue. "But you're not sure yet," she said.

"Well, not one hundred percent," he admitted.

"So maybe you're wrong," the girl said.

He smiled. "I could be, but I wouldn't put too much hope on it if I were you. With modern technology, we'll be able to find out the truth once and for all." He said goodbye with a nod. But before he left, he added, "No need to secretly follow me anymore. I can answer questions you have whenever you want." Then he walked off, whistling.

Standing there watching him, the three friends felt completely discouraged. They sat down in a spot that had a wonderful view of the Tintagel ridge. The ruins of the castle sat on a piece of land that stuck out from the cliff. It was surrounded by turquoise-green seawater, and to get there, you had to walk a narrow path. Then you had to cross a small bridge and take a steep set of stairs. But once you were at the top, you could enjoy a breathtaking view of the cliffs. And if you looked down during low tide, you could see the entrance of Merlin's mysterious cave.

It was a truly fascinating and magical place.

"Could Tristam be right? Is Merlin's cave a fake?" asked Thomasina, putting her chin on her hands.

"I don't trust what Mr. Perfect-Hair says," grumbled Minerva.

"But Tristam is a famous archaeologist," said Ravi. "And he's using some scientific tools."

"Don't you guys remember what Agatha said?" Minerva asked. "There's much more in this world than what you see. We just have to look for it!"

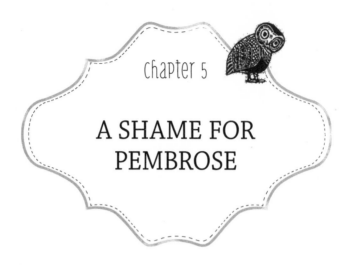

chapter 5

A SHAME FOR PEMBROSE

The team of experts with their scientific instruments completed their inspections of Merlin's cave. As predicted, Tristam declared that it was a fake — a tourist trap. In short, the famous sorcerer's cave did not exist.

The archaeologist made his official announcement in front of the whole town, just two days after his conversation with the Order of the Owls. It was almost evening, and Pembrose villagers had gathered by the port to watch a performance by the amateur dramatic society.

"I'm sorry to let you all down," said the young archaeologist, tilting his head to highlight his blond hair. "But science doesn't lie."

The villagers did not welcome his announcement.

"This is a loss for the village!" Dr. Gerald said.

"Right when the tourist season was about to start!" the vicar said, sighing.

"I knew it. Nothing good comes from London," said Ms. Haddok to the person next to her.

Ravi, Minerva, and Thomasina were sitting at their usual place by the dock and dangling their feet in the water.

"Could he be lying?" Ravi asked Minerva.

Minerva moved her toes inside her rubber boots. She stretched and bent them to see if they tickled — that would be a dead giveaway that Tristam was lying.

"No, I don't feel a thing!" she said after several tries.

"Not even a little tickle?" asked Thomasina, full of hope.

Minerva took her boots off and dangled her feet. She waited a bit just to be sure. "No. He's telling the truth," she said dully.

"Shoot, then he won," said Ravi.

"No!" insisted Minerva. "There must be another reason for sure." She glared at the archaeologist. As usual, he was surrounded by the single ladies of Pembrose, who were all fighting for his attention.

"Tristam Hope-His-Hair-Falls-Out will have to eat his words!"

* * *

That night was very restless for the people of Pembrose. Their heads tossed and turned on their pillows without rest. It was not easy to fall asleep knowing that the village would probably be forgotten

now that Merlin's cave had been exposed as a fake. They would have to face the shame of all the tourist guides cancelling their visits!

The clouds rolled through the sky, and the wind blew down the cobblestone paths. It went under the doors and touched the faces of the girls who were dreaming about Tristam the handsome.

The wind blew in the heath moor, too, down the chimney of Agatha's house, where embers glowed orange. Only Pendragon was still awake, barking at the moon.

The wind blew on Tintagel Castle, which rested silently, surrounded by its history. Waves broke against the cliffs below. Tristam camped nearby. He rested peacefully, unaware he had caused such a stir.

The wind blew on Admiral Rock, making the walls of Lizard Manor squeak. Safe indoors, Minerva slept inside her yellow tent. She dreamed about the heath moor with crimson heather and the little, blue lake where she swam with Thomasina. As she slept, she held the small flute that belonged to her parents tightly in her hands. Mrs. Flopps snored in the Widow's Room, on the second floor. She dreamed about seaside landscapes that she would paint with many shades of blue. The moon was just a slice hanging from the sky. It projected a thin ray of light into her room.

The owls on the roof, on the other hand, could see even in darkness. Their yellow eyes faced the trees that whispered like ghosts.

CHAPTER 6

THE HEATH MOOR WITCH

The next morning, Minerva decided something. She flew out of her yellow tent with determination and ran downstairs in a hurry.

Mrs. Flopps was drinking her first cup of tea for the day in kitchen number three. A pie, fresh from the oven, sat on the table.

Minerva grabbed a slice and folded her legs under her on a chair. The wind had swept away all the clouds in the sky, and the sun shone brightly through the window.

Minerva bit into the pie eagerly. There were plenty of things to do that day. The Order of the Owls had to prove to everyone that Merlin really existed!

Mrs. Flopps was already dressed. Like Minerva, she found her clothing in Lizard Manor's chests and closets. That day, she was wearing a white blouse with a high neckline that was closed with a pin, along with a tweed jacket and skirt. Her gray hair was done up in an elegant bun. And on top of her head, she wore a small, girly hat.

Minerva's hair, on the other hand, was crazier than ever, spreading all over like tentacles. Her hair seemed to express her thoughts; Minerva's mind was completely restless!

Mrs. Flopps looked at her in surprise. Minerva was usually very talkative in the morning. But today she was sitting quietly, her legs folded neatly beneath her.

"Everything all right?" Mrs. Flopps asked, swallowing her last sip of tea.

Minerva didn't answer. Her freckled face was full of concentration.

"Well," said Mrs. Flopps casually, "I'm going out to paint." She got up, making the chair squeak, and walked out.

Minerva didn't even realize Mrs. Flopps had left. With all her thinking, she had finally come to a conclusion. She knew that the cave was not the right one. So there was just one solution — they had to find Merlin's real cave!

Minerva was sure it existed. They just needed to look harder. And she knew just the person who could help them.

Having made this important decision, she ran a hand through her hair and realized that it really needed to be brushed. She hurried out of the kitchen, pausing a moment to decide which of the nine bathrooms to use that day. Finally, she picked number five for its wonderful view of the sea.

* * *

Minerva was so anxious to tell her friends about her idea that she didn't have the patience to wait for them to come to Lizard Manor that afternoon. She knew that Ravi always gave Thomasina a ride after school, so when her friends arrived at the post office, she was already there, waiting impatiently.

"The Order of the Owls has a very important mission!" she announced before her friends even had time to put their feet on the ground.

Thomasina easily jumped off the bike. Her school uniform, which usually made all the girls look horrible, looked wonderful on her. "Tell me what it is!" she begged.

Ravi, who still hadn't entirely gotten over the events of the fox hunt, mumbled, "Oh, no . . ." His voice was so low that the girls did not hear him.

"The cave under Tintagel Castle isn't the right one!" said Minerva, all excited. "But I'm positive that Merlin's real cave is nearby. We just have to find it."

"You're right! Why didn't I think of that?" said Thomasina. "Let's go find it right away!"

"And how do you think you're going to find it?" said Ravi. "Do you think it's on a map?"

"You're so negative!" said Thomasina, frowning.

"And you don't think things through enough!" responded Ravi.

They started to argue, and Minerva, as usual, had to interrupt to make them stop.

"Be quiet!" she yelled.

Ravi and Thomasina shut up.

"I know who can help us," said Minerva. "Agatha. She knows everything about Arthur and Merlin. We must go to her house in the heath moor."

Ravi felt a shiver down his spine. "You want to go to Alder Swamp?" he uttered. "How is it possible with just one bicycle? It's too far . . ."

"Right . . . I didn't think about that," said Minerva, slightly discouraged.

Right then, a truck full of produce stopped in front of the post office. Bert, a farmer who lived in Bodmin Heath Moor, was delivering something to Ravi's mom.

Minerva lit up. "We can ask Bert to drive us there,"

she said. "He should know where Agatha lives. They must be neighbors."

So, after reassuring Mrs. Kapoor that they would only be away for a couple of hours, they got in the back of the truck and sat among the cases of produce.

The road to Alder Swamp was full of rocks and holes, and the three children kept bouncing in the air. Minerva and Thomasina enjoyed it, but the same could not be said for Ravi.

The boy sat with his arms crossed the whole time, thinking how awful girls could be. Even if they were beautiful.

And they haven't even thought about how we're going to get back, he thought.

Bert left them at a crossroads in the middle of nowhere, where they were blown away by a cold wind. All they could see for miles was heather and rocky hills all around them. From behind one of the hills, though, a thin stream of smoke arose.

"Let's go there!" decided Minerva.

Indeed, the smoke was from Agatha's cottage. The little home seemed ancient. It was made of dark stone, with grass and moss growing between the rocks. The roof was made of straw, and pots filled with pink flowers sat on the windowsill. A vegetable garden sat on one side of the cottage, and a roost full of chickens sat on the other side.

As soon as they opened the front gate, they heard a furious bark. A moment later Pendragon came at them as fast as a missile.

The noise drew Agatha's attention to the door. "Oh, how nice. You came to see me!" she shouted, waving one hand to greet them.

They couldn't say a thing back, because Pendragon had pushed them over and was furiously licking their faces.

* * *

The cottage was very cozy on the inside; it didn't look like a witch's cove at all. Agatha put some water on the fireplace to boil for tea, and she toasted some thick slices of bread. On the table, there were a block of butter and a jar of heather honey. Agatha had also baked a cinnamon pie, which filled the room with its intense smell.

After devouring everything, Ravi, Minerva, and Thomasina sat on the floor by the fireplace, with Pendragon lying across their stomachs. They took turns telling Agatha what had happened.

Agatha sat in a wooden chair with a high seat-back. As she listened, she sewed, an activity that helped her think.

When the trio's story was finished, she rested her sewing on her lap. She had a small wrinkle in the middle of her forehead, and her big blue eyes were deep in thought.

"So, can you help us?" asked Minerva.

Agatha sighed. "Waking up old legends is dangerous," she said. "You never know what will happen. Sometimes the past is better left alone."

"But it's so important for the villagers to find out where Merlin's cave really is," Minerva said.

"Everyone's so disappointed," added Ravi. He liked Agatha, and her house was not as scary as he had imagined. Maybe the adventure that Minerva and Thomasina had dragged him into wouldn't be as crazy as the others.

All three of them were so insistent that Agatha gave in. "Okay," she said. "What do you guys want to know?"

"Tell us more about Merlin!" said Minerva.

Agatha stirred the fireplace ashes. Then, standing over the flames, as if she could read the fire, she started: "I've already told you that he was the son of a very powerful fairy, haven't I?"

The children nodded, already captured by the tale.

"Yes, and the night he was born there were some bad signs . . ." said Minerva.

"And the moon became red," continued Ravi, looking at Agatha.

"Because his birth was out of the ordinary," said Agatha. "Merlin showed extraordinary gifts even as a boy. He was a witty child, and he liked to tease everyone with riddles and charades. Everything he said was hard to understand. He spent a lot of time alone, because his mother, the fairy, had abandoned him and his father was too afraid to be around him. Then Merlin took refuge in a cove on the coast, where he practiced his magic —"

"The cave!" the three said excitedly.

"Exactly," said Agatha with a smile. "Some believed he was bad. But he wasn't; he simply had above-average intelligence. For this reason, his peers were frightened of him. They were envious, too. Soon enough Merlin realized he was a shapeshifter."

The reflection of the flames was dancing on the woman's face, creating lights and shades.

"What's a shapeshifter?" asked Minerva.

"Merlin could change into any animal he wanted," answered Agatha.

"Wow!" said Thomasina. "If I could do that, I'd change into a dolphin!"

"I'd be an albatross and fly to India!" said Ravi.

Minerva didn't know what she wanted to become yet. There were so many possibilities.

Agatha smiled. "It was a very useful gift. Merlin became almost invincible. He was so powerful that no one dared to challenge him. Arthur was born and became king with the help of Merlin's magic. And the sorcerer always remained King Arthur's most faithful counselor."

"So the cave must be close to the castle," said Minerva. "Do you know where it is?"

Agatha stood up. She picked up a shawl from the back of the chair and put it around her shoulders. "Follow me," she said, calling Pendragon along, too.

Outside the wind had become very crisp. Agatha led the others along the path close to the swamp, down to an open space where twelve big rocks were set in a circle.

Agatha went over to the smallest one and leaned over it. The three friends got closer, while Pendragon jumped all around them.

Agatha swept debris and dust off the rock with her hand. "There's an inscription," she said. "See it?"

They leaned in to take a look. "What language is that?" asked Ravi. "They look like signs."

"They're runes, an old Nordic language used by sorcerers," explained Agatha. "*Rune* means *secret*." She pointed to the circle of rocks. "This circle is ancient. It's used to set the positions of planets and stars. It was built long before Merlin was born. People say that he came here on every summer solstice to observe the stars. Do you see this symbol at the end of the inscription?" she asked.

"Yes," answered Ravi. "It looks like a cane with a rounded knob."

"It's Merlin's symbol. It means wisdom," said Agatha.

"So did he carve these runes himself?" said Thomasina.

"Yes. And they could help you figure out where his cave is."

"Do you know what they mean?" asked Minerva.

Agatha shook her head. "Unfortunately I don't. You need to ask an expert."

Ravi and Thomasina looked discouraged. Once again, they had a problem.

But Minerva wasn't going to get discouraged that easily. "That just means we have to find an expert!" She asked Thomasina, "Do you have a pen and a piece of paper in your purse? That way we can copy the inscription."

Her friend nodded. Pulling a notepad and a pencil from her purse, she copied the runes with great precision — one by one. "Done," she said finally, putting the notepad away.

Agatha gave them a ride back to the village in her

Jeep. Before they got out, she put one hand in her pocket and pulled out a small cloth bag with a blue ribbon. She handed the bag to Minerva. "Here. But beware, don't open it until it's the right time."

Minerva looked at her, a bit confused.

"Don't worry, you'll understand," Agatha reassured her.

Minerva gave it to Thomasina. "Keep it in your purse."

After taking turns petting Pendragon goodbye, they all got out of the Jeep.

Agatha leaned out the window. She hesitated, then said, "Merlin was a clairvoyant. That means he could predict the future," she said. "He had already foreseen many things. His cave was a secret place, and no one was allowed to enter. So, if you find it, be very careful! Merlin knew many tricks."

Ravi shivered. He was positive they would all end up in trouble once again!

Agatha started the engine, but before leaving, she leaned out the window once more. "One last piece of advice," she yelled over Pendragon's barking. "Don't touch the monkey for any reason!"

Ravi, Thomasina, and Minerva stood there looking at the car as it drove away. They weren't sure they'd heard Agatha right.

"Monkey?" asked Ravi. "Are there any monkeys in Cornwall?"

CHAPTER 7

TINTAGEL'S GHOST

Thomasina wrinkled her forehead and studied the notepad with the inscription of the runes.

"Can you translate runes now?" Ravi asked sarcastically.

"No," she said, closing the pad. "We could go work on it at my house. There are a lot of dictionaries in the library . . ."

"No way!" Ravi immediately stopped her. "Not after what happened at your house the last time."

"Oh, I don't see why you got so upset," said Thomasina.

"Everything turned out fine, and we saved the fox in the end, didn't we?" Minerva reminded him.

"Yeah, but we're lucky they didn't find out what I did. The hunters would have tried to teach me a lesson! Did you think about that?"

Thomasina shrugged her shoulders. "It's part of the adventure," she said.

Meanwhile Minerva was thinking again. They were still standing right where Agatha had left them, on Pembrose's main road, unsure of what to do.

The bell tower struck five and Ms. Haddok, Dr. Gerald's nurse, came out of the clinic at the end of the road. Today's visits were finished.

Minerva got an idea. "Hey, guys, I know who we can ask to translate the runes!" she said.

Ravi and Thomasina immediately stopped arguing and turned to Minerva.

"Dr. Gerald! Do you remember? He was the one who told us *Ordo Noctuae* means *Order of the Owls*. If he knows Latin, maybe he knows the runes as well."

"You're right!" Thomasina said. "Dr. Gerald knows

a lot of things. Everyone goes to him when they have a problem."

The three of them walked toward the doctor's office, but after a couple of steps Tristam crossed their path. He was looking down and was in a hurry. "Oh, I'm sorry," he said. "I didn't see you."

"I bet you didn't. You should look where you're going!" said Ravi.

Instead of answering, Tristam jumped behind them and begged, "Please, hide me!"

Ms. Araminta Bartholomew got there in a hurry, her cheeks flushed. She was wearing a very elegant dress. She looked around, mumbling to herself, "I wonder . . . where did he go?" then kept going.

When she was gone, Tristam came out of his hiding spot. "That was close," he said, sighing.

The children looked at him, puzzled.

"I know you three don't like me, but thanks anyway for your help," he said. "You see, Araminta wanted to invite me over for tea, but I . . . let's just say I have other commitments."

"Right," said Minerva. "You're really busy destroying the reputation of our village."

"Or maybe you want to prove that even Arthur didn't exist," said Thomasina.

"I'm sorry that you are all so upset," said Tristam, sounding more like his usual know-it-all self. "I told you, I wish I could believe in legends and magic myself, but I'm a scientist. I only believe in what can be proven."

"Well, then we're going to prove you're wrong!" said Minerva.

The archaeologist smiled. "Really?" He crossed his arms and looked at them with interest. "You guys are pretty determined, no doubt about that. But you don't have much time."

"What do you mean?" asked Minerva.

"There's going to be a press conference the day after tomorrow," said Tristam. "I will officially announce that the cave underneath Tintagel Castle didn't belong to Merlin. And Pembrose's name will disappear from tourist guides."

"So soon?" asked Thomasina.

"Yes. I have to go back to London. I have no reason to stay here anymore . . ." Tristam hesitated for a moment and his eyes sparked.

Minerva noticed it. She remembered the archaeologist's strange behavior, how he often wandered around the village as if he was looking for someone.

He babbled, "Isn't it . . ." He stopped. "No, nothing. It's nothing." He ran his hand through his hair like usual. He was lost in thought. "The thing is . . . while I was taking care of my research in Tintagel, I saw a girl. And well, she was extremely beautiful," he added with embarrassment. "It was very early, almost sunrise, and the castle ruins were surrounded by fog, so I'm not sure I saw it right. She had a peculiar face, and her eyes were like the sky."

"Maybe she was the ghost of a lady who lived in the castle centuries ago," suggested Minerva. "Oh, wait, I forgot. You don't believe in ghosts, do you? They're not very scientific."

"Oh, forget about it!" said Tristam, upset. "I knew it was nothing."

"Okay. Now if you'll excuse us, we have an important commitment," said Thomasina in her parents' smug tone.

"Yeah, a very important commitment," added Ravi.

"And we'll prove you wrong!" said Minerva. "Mr. Handsome-Floppy-Hair," she added in a low voice.

But Tristam heard what she said. "Be my guests. But remember, time is running out!" he said bowing deeply. He was back to his usual self again. "I like challenges," he added with a wink. And off he went, whistling.

Ravi, Minerva, and Thomasina looked at one another.

"What are we waiting for?" asked Minerva. "The Order of the Owls can't waste a single second!"

They hurried to the doctor's office and knocked on the door.

No one answered.

"Let's hope the doctor didn't leave yet, even though office hours are over," said Ravi. Finding Merlin's cave had now become very important to him — just so they could show it to Tristam.

They knocked even harder, pounding their fists on the door.

The doctor finally opened the door. He looked at them, confused. "Office hours are over now," he said. "You can make an appointment with my nurse tomorrow."

Dr. Gerald was tall — so tall that he often had to bend over to avoid hitting doorframes and low ceilings. He was the only one in town who always wore a tie, and he was popular among older women. They would often show up at his office, even if they were perfectly healthy, just to gossip with his nurse and drink tea. He had learned to avoid people who bothered him. For this reason, he was looking at the group suspiciously. After taking a good look at them, though, he decided they looked flushed and anxious.

"Are you guys sick?" he asked, concerned.

"Well, in a way," said Thomasina.

The doctor looked at her with a serious face. "Miss, one is either sick or not sick."

"Well, we're definitely not sick," said Ravi.

"But we have a problem," Minerva added.

The doctor sighed and let them in. "Come in, or we'll be here all night."

They followed him to his office. He sat down behind a heavy desk and told them to sit down. Dr. Gerald's office was filled with books. He was the most educated man in the village. He knew Greek and Latin, and when he was not seeing patients, he was reading. Currently, there was a book on his desk with a cheese sandwich stuck inside to keep track of the page.

They must have come at a bad time.

"So, what can I do for you?" asked the doctor, sitting back in his chair.

They were sitting on the edge of their chairs, a bit embarrassed. Thomasina took the notepad out of her purse. She opened it to the page with the runes and handed it to the doctor.

He put his glasses on and examined the page. "Ah, runes!" he said.

"Yes," said Minerva. "Could you tell us what they mean, please?"

The doctor went to grab a big book from the shelf. "Are you studying runes in school?" he asked.

"Yes," answered Ravi immediately. "I mean, no!" he added quickly, noticing that Minerva was shuffling her feet and turning red. "It's more of a hobby . . ."

"Okay, okay," mumbled the doctor, examining the runes. "Mmm, very interesting . . ."

"Really?" said Ravi.

"What does it say?" asked Thomasina impatiently.

"Mmm, just a second . . ."

"What is it!?" said Minerva.

The doctor took off his glasses and looked at them. "Well, it doesn't make any sense!"

CHAPTER 8

MERLIN, WHAT A FUNNY CHAP!

Three pairs of eyes stared intently at the pad of paper. Three pairs of feet moved nervously. A cloud of frustration filled the air.

Ravi, Minerva, and Thomasina were lying on their stomachs in Lizard Manor's yard with the notepad in the middle of them.

They had been staring at that pad of paper for hours. At least it seemed that way to Ravi.

Seven owls watched them from the roof. Evidently, they found the scene rather amusing. They moved their soft-feathered heads up and down, as if they were laughing.

The children had studied Merlin's mysterious message the night before. Then they met to work on it some more at Minerva's house after school. But after hours of thinking, they hadn't gotten anywhere. Not even a big snack made a difference; the only help that it offered was a jam stain on the notepad.

"Read it again," Ravi told Thomasina. "Maybe if we hear it out loud, it will be easier to understand what it says."

She cleared her throat and read, "'The entrance is invisible to the giant. Get up, looking at the sea. Go left and you'll be wrong for sure.'"

Ravi shook his head and rolled over onto his back. "I give up!" he yelled.

Minerva didn't say a word. She just stared at the paper with a wrinkled forehead. She played with her hair, and it soon became a crazy ball.

"Who is this giant?" asked Thomasina.

"And why do we care about him?" added Ravi.

"Dr. Gerald is right," said Thomasina. "This message doesn't make any sense."

"Then it was Merlin who wrote it," said Ravi. "Agatha told us that he liked tricking everyone."

Minerva suddenly jumped up in the air, scaring her friends to death. "A riddle!" she yelled. "Why didn't I think of that sooner?" Full of excitement, she looked at them.

"Are you okay?" Ravi asked her. "Did something bite you?"

Minerva shook her head. Her freckled face was sparkling with a smile. "I'm great. Come with me!" she yelled, running toward her house.

"Do we have to?" asked Ravi. Lizard Manor was not one of his favorite places.

Thomasina grabbed his arm and dragged him toward the entrance. "Come on, don't act like that!"

Lizard Manor was dark, as usual. Lightbulbs constantly went out in the old mansion, and Minerva and Mrs. Flopps could not figure out why. So they just used candles and oil lamps. Ravi bumped into the suit of armor at the entrance and then into the edge of a chest before his eyes adjusted to the darkness. Next he felt something sliding across his ankle. He wasn't sure if it was one of the foxes or Hugo the badger or, worst of the worst, a lizard!

Minerva led her friends to the library, where it was easy to see; plenty of light streamed in from the big windows in the room. Bookshelves, running from floor to ceiling, covered all four walls, including the spaces between the windows.

"Don't touch anything," Minerva warned them. "Most of the books are very old and if you aren't careful, they crumble."

Minerva went toward the desk where she usually studied, or tried to. "I've started reading Arthur and the Knights of the Round Table's history," she explained. "In this book, there's a map of the area around Tintagel."

She gently opened the leather-covered volume. The pages had that nice smell of old paper.

"Here, look," she said, pointing to the map. "This is the castle surrounded by cliffs."

Their heads lowered over the piece of paper.

"What should we look for?" asked Ravi.

Minerva moved her finger on the page. "If I'm right, there should be . . . there it is!" she said. "Giant Rock! It's very close to Tintagel."

"Ah!" said Ravi. "The giant is not a person, but a place."

"I don't understand," said Thomasina. "Even if it's a place, the sentence says that the entrance is invisible to the giant."

"That's right, but it's one of Merlin's riddles," Minerva explained. "We have to do exactly the opposite of what he says."

"Wow, genius!" Thomasina said.

Ravi took the notepad in his hands and read: "'The entrance is invisible to the giant. Get up, looking at the sea. Go left and you'll be wrong for sure.' So, it means that from the cliff you can see the entrance. Right?"

Thomasina interrupted him: "We have to go to Giant Rock, go down without looking at the sea, and go right . . . don't we?"

"Yes!" shouted Minerva, nodding.

Thomasina took the notepad and put it back in her purse. "So, what are we waiting for?" she asked.

"You want to go now?" asked Ravi.

"Good idea," Minerva said. "Tristam will make his announcement tomorrow. We shouldn't waste any time."

"Are you planning to walk there?" asked Ravi. "It will take forever."

"Come on, lazy. Giant Rock isn't that far away!" Minerva said, encouraging him.

Ravi swallowed. How high was Giant Rock? Too high, he was sure of it. And he was terribly afraid of heights. But that was one thing his crush, Thomasina, did not need to know. So he just said, "Okay," his voice a bit shaky. He was hoping he would be lucky . . . for once.

CHAPTER 9

DON'T TRUST THE MONKEY!

They prepared for their adventure. They expected it to be dark inside the cave, so they each brought a flashlight. Next they grabbed some old sweaters and a change of clothes for each of them from one of Lizard Manor's closets. They put everything in a backpack. In no time at all, they were ready to leave.

The three friends practically ran on the coastline path. The days were getting longer and it was still light out. But not for long. The sun was already low, and the seagulls were making their last circles to look for fish before going back into their nests.

"Here, this is the place!" Thomasina said when they reached the point that Minerva's map called Giant Rock. She pulled the binoculars from her purse and looked around. The view was breathtaking. "Down there!" she said.

She pointed to a rocky island. Turquoise water washed across a thin strip of land that connected the island to the mainland. Tintagel, where the fake cave was, was just a few hundred yards away, on the shore.

"Come on, let's go down!" said Minerva.

Ravi looked. The path down was very steep and narrow. Worst of all, it was set among sharp rocks.

Minerva turned her shoulders to the sea and started to go down behind Thomasina.

"How do you know this is the right direction?" asked Ravi.

"I don't know," Minerva answered. "But we have to follow Merlin's instructions."

"Yeah, too bad he enjoyed tricking people!" said Ravi.

"Stop complaining," said Minerva. "I'll hold on to Thomasina, and she'll hold on to you, so you'll be last. Happy?"

The friends started to go down slowly, with their hands on each other's shoulders. They walked backward, looking like a train going the wrong way. Every now and then, one of them moved a rock with his or her feet, sending it into the sea, dozens of feet below them.

Ravi's walk was a little shaky because he was wearing the backpack on his stomach so that Thomasina could put her hands on his shoulders. He squeezed his eyes closed. But he was afraid to end up like the rocks, so he opened them again. That was when he noticed an opening in the rocks just to his right.

"Hey, what's that?" he asked.

His friends stopped.

Thomasina bent over and tried to look inside the tunnel. "I see a light down there. It could be a shortcut! And the instructions said go left —"

"So we have to go right," interrupted Minerva.

"We're on the right path!" said Thomasina enthusiastically.

They went inside the tunnel on their hands and knees and crawled a few dozen feet. They came out on a small beach of pebbles and cliffs, washed by fluffy waves. That was where the strip of land that connected to the island started. It was as thin as a piece of rope.

"We'll have to walk like acrobats," said Thomasina. "Keep your arms out and put one foot in front of the other."

It took the girls mere seconds to get to the other side. Meanwhile, Ravi was stalling on the beach. He still hadn't told his friends that he couldn't swim.

"What are you waiting for?" Thomasina called to him. "The tide is rising. We don't have much time!"

Ravi held his breath and ran across without looking. He miraculously found himself on the other side and started to breathe again. He was relieved to have that over with.

"Let's split up to find the entrance to the cave," Minerva said.

Ravi found it first. The entrance was in the shape of a snake, and it was so narrow that an adult would have a hard time getting through it.

The girls slid inside without hesitation. Ravi followed them but with caution. He was thinking about Agatha's warning: Merlin didn't like other people in his cave. He had many tricks to discourage visitors. What would they find on the other side?

Well, nothing special. The hole was rather narrow, and there was nothing much to see — just a small waterfall that had eroded the rock.

Even Ravi was disappointed. He was starting to actually enjoy the adventure. "This is nothing special for a powerful sorcerer's cave!" he said, sitting down on a round rock.

Thomasina turned on a flashlight and pointed it toward the humid walls, full of seaweed and shells. She was clearly frustrated.

"So much work for nothing!" said Ravi. He was

a bit grateful for Thomasina's disappointment. Now she would understand that some thought was needed before starting a new adventure.

Minerva wasn't ready to give up, though. She started to touch the walls.

"Do you expect to find a secret entrance?" asked Ravi sarcastically.

Minerva ignored him and got closer to the waterfall, stepping inside the water with her boots. She stretched her arms through, and since she could not feel rock on the other side, she put her head inside the stream, too. She immediately pulled back and yelled, "Come here! There's an opening behind this!"

"Wait!" Ravi got up to join her, but she had already disappeared beyond the waterfall.

"Wow!" yelled Thomasina. She disappeared behind Minerva.

Ravi raised his eyes to the sky and followed his friends.

Behind the waterfall, they found a natural steep staircase between two narrow walls. And this time they were not let down. A wonderful world was unveiled to them. The cave was huge. The lights from the three flashlights lit the majestic rock walls, which came together up high in a vault. This ceiling was supported by several pillars made of stalactites and stalagmites, a result of the constant dripping of water through the centuries. A number of bats hung from the vaulted ceiling. In some areas, the rock had a mineral that sparkled in the darkness, so it looked like the bats were suspended in a sky full of stars.

Openings to various tunnels lined the walls. "Where should we go now?" asked Minerva, puzzled. "Which pathway should we choose?"

"And, above all, how can we avoid getting lost?" added Ravi.

"I know," said Thomasina. She took a piece of white chalk from her purse and traced a number one at the entrance of the biggest tunnel. "Let's start here."

Minerva was amazed. "That's perfect!" she said. "Every time we turn or change direction, we'll write a number on the rock so we can find our way back. We won't get lost," she said, winking at Ravi.

"Right, good idea . . ." he admitted. He led his friends into the tunnel.

The cave was so big and the wonders so many that the friends felt like they were explorers in a new world. Before they realized it, hours had passed.

"Hey, what time is it?" asked Ravi suddenly. They had just reached a second hole even bigger than the first one.

"Eight," answered Thomasina, checking her fancy watch with the sparkly face.

Ravi put a hand on his forehead. "Ugh, high tide!" he said. "We have to get out of here, or we'll have to stay on the island! We can't stay here all night. We can come back tomorrow with Tristam. Then he'll be able to study the cave and take care of his analysis."

Minerva wanted to keep going, but Thomasina hesitated. She was worried about what her parents would say if she didn't come home.

Finally, Thomasina said, "Okay, let's go. But we'll

come back right away tomorrow morning before school."

They went backward, following the numbers they had drawn with the chalk. But when they emerged at the opening of the rock, they found that the island had been completely surrounded by the sea.

"Too late!" said Minerva.

"Oh, no!" Ravi looked around in despair. The currents were very strong, and fluffy waves broke against the rocks. It was unthinkable to swim to the shore, especially in the darkness. And also because he couldn't swim. "I think we'll have to spend the night on the island," he said, sighing. He hoped that his mom would think that he was spending the night at Minerva's. He didn't want her to worry.

Thomasina, on the other hand, had already forgotten about her parents. She wasn't concerned because she was very good at avoiding punishment. "While we're at it, what do you say we keep exploring the cave?" she asked.

"Right!" agreed Minerva. "So tomorrow we can

show Tristam that he was wrong!" She was sure that Mrs. Flopps wouldn't worry about her. The woman knew Minerva could take care of herself in any circumstance.

Minerva didn't notice the pair of round yellow eyes on her. A big white owl was sitting on a rock, watching the island.

They were not alone after all.

* * *

Minerva, Thomasina, and Ravi journeyed back into the cave, going through the passage under the waterfall for the third time. They decided to follow a different tunnel, because the cavity they had reached before turning around didn't hold anything interesting.

Thomasina traced a number each time they turned. After a few hundred feet, they reached a third hole. They stood in the middle and pointed the flashlights all around in astonishment. At the bottom of the stalactite and stalagmite pillars, someone had carved animals! There were so many: a lion, a dolphin, a turtle, a cat, a bull, an ermine, a horse . . .

Ravi looked closely at a hare's face. "Wow, it's like a stone zoo!"

"Well, Merlin was a shapeshifter," Minerva said thoughtfully. "These could all be animals he changed himself into."

Thomasina pointed the flashlight on a deer. "What if one of these sculptures was hiding something? Something that Merlin wouldn't want us to find?"

"You're right!" said Minerva. "He enjoyed riddles. Which of these animals could he have chosen to hide a secret?"

Ravi moved toward a pillar. "Well, Merlin was spiteful and he made fun of everyone," he said. "Maybe the monkey —"

"NO!" yelled Minerva.

"Remember what Agatha told us!" Thomasina added, trying to stop him. But it was too late. Ravi had just touched the monkey's head — the only animal he was not supposed to touch!

A trap went off immediately. The rock beneath their feet opened up, and they fell into the void. Fortunately, they fell into a salt lake with a big splash.

Minerva and Thomasina's heads quickly popped up from the water.

"Ugh! Of course he had to touch the monkey!" said Thomasina. She spit out the water she had swallowed and began to swim toward the lakeshore. "Now we're really in trouble..."

"Wait, I can't see Ravi!" shouted Minerva, who was still in the water.

Thomasina immediately went back and dove under with Minerva. Luckily, the lake was not deep. They found the boy and brought him to the surface.

Ravi gasped, trying to catch his breath. "Help me!" he shouted. "I can't swim! I didn't tell you, but I can't swim! Help! Help!"

"Relax, we've got you," Minerva said, trying to reassure him. "I'm a swimming champion."

They dragged him to the shore, where he lay gasping. "Wow, that was close!"

"Yeah, because you didn't follow Agatha's advice!" Thomasina reminded him.

"I forgot . . ." Ravi said. "Anyway, *you* dragged us here!"

"Everything was great before you put us in trouble!" Thomasina answered back. "And you could have told us that you can't swim. There's nothing wrong with it."

"It's none of your business."

"Ah, really? Well, then next time you nearly drown, it's going to be none of my business!"

While they argued, Minerva looked up at the opening that they had fallen out of. It was too high to reach. And the lake, even if it was shallow, was so big that she couldn't see the other side in the dark. The only thing around the small shore was a wall of rocks.

"Guys," she said, "instead of arguing, let's focus on figuring out how to get out of here!"

Ravi and Thomasina shut up.

Minerva pointed the flashlight all around, shining on the entrances of several galleries that opened at different heights. Here, too, bats hung from the vault.

"Which way should we go?" she asked.

Unfortunately, they did not have Thomasina's chalk numbers to tell them the right direction to take.

Ravi was still panting. "Oh, no! We're going to be stuck here forever!"

It seemed there was no other solution than picking up a place to start from and hoping it was the right one.

But how many possibilities did they have to find the way back? It seemed like too many.

"Darn sorcerer and his sense of humor!" said Ravi, falling on the sand.

CHAPTER 10

AN UNEXPECTED HELP

Thankfully, the things they had in the backpack were still dry, so they changed. The old clothes smelled a little like mothballs, but at least they were warm. The temperature was dropping, so they put on the sweaters as well.

When their teeth stopped chattering, they tried to think of a solution. But all that happened was Ravi and Thomasina started to argue again, blaming each other, while Minerva tried to come up with a plan to get out of their situation.

All of a sudden, they heard a loud rumble that

made everyone shake. "What was that?" asked Thomasina, looking worried.

Ravi put his hands on his stomach. "It's my stomach," he said, embarrassed. "Does anyone have anything to eat? I'm so hungry."

Thomasina smiled a bit, opened her precious purse, and grabbed three big bars of chocolate. "Here you go!"

"Wow!" said Ravi, taking one. "Thomasina, you're wonderful! I love you!" That last bit slipped out before he could stop himself. He blushed, trying to hide his embarrassment by chomping into the chocolate.

The truce held for a while, but when the effects of the chocolate wore off and the hunger pains grew stronger, they all started arguing again. They couldn't make a decision. If they picked the wrong direction, they could be trapped inside the cave forever.

After a while, tired from all the adventures of the day, their eyelids became heavy. Ravi fell asleep first. Thomasina tried to wake him, but then she, too, grew tired and fell asleep next to him.

Minerva, on the other hand, stayed awake thinking. She kept lighting the cave walls with her flashlight, trying to find something that told her which way to go. But finally, she fell asleep as well. When she woke up a little bit later, she found herself on her back with the flashlight pointing to the ceiling. She realized the light on the ceiling bothered the bats. Some of them flew away. She pointed the light elsewhere and other bats detached themselves from the rocky vault, flying toward the same direction.

"Guys!" shouted Minerva, waking up the others. She had an idea.

"What?" asked Ravi, sitting up.

"Huh?" said Thomasina, rubbing her eyes.

"Do what I do. Turn on the flashlights and point them toward the ceiling!" yelled Minerva.

Ravi and Thomasina did what Minerva told them. Hundreds of bats immediately detached themselves from the vault and flew in the same direction. Minerva followed them with her light. They flew into a gallery that was just a couple feet from where they were.

"Come on, let's follow them!" she yelled.

They climbed into the gallery.

"Keep shining the light at them. I bet they'll lead us out," said Minerva.

They started running after the bats, bombarding them with light from the flashlights.

The bats flew all around the three friends. They turned down another tunnel and then another one. It was like a maze, and the Order of Owls soon found themselves short of breath. They came to a stop.

"I can't do this anymore!" said Ravi.

Minerva leaned against a wall to catch her breath.

Thomasina tried to push them, "Come on, we can't give up now, we're almost there! And . . ."

"Look!" yelled Minerva, pointing in front of them.

The bats were all entering an opening. A thin ray of light from the moon shone through it, lighting the bats as they flew through. The three children waited for the last bat to leave, then they got closer and looked up.

"If we get on top of each other, we'll be able to reach it," said Thomasina.

They stayed there, their noses upward, watching the opening for a while. The sky, full of stars, was very inviting after the darkness of the cave.

Ravi made a decision. "I'm the tallest," he said. "Thomasina, get on my shoulders. Minerva, you're the shortest and lightest so you get on last."

Putting one foot in Ravi's hand, Thomasina climbed on without a problem. Then she stretched one arm and helped her friend up. Minerva pushed herself through the opening. She emerged on the island, not far from the cave entrance, and pulled Thomasina up after her. Then after several tries, Ravi managed to climb high enough to grab Minerva and Thomasina's arms.

The three of them sat down and breathed the fresh night air. They let themselves rock to the rhythm of the waves breaking against the cliffs.

No one knew exactly what time it was, because Thomasina's watch had stopped working after she fell in the water. But the moon was almost gone, so sunrise was about to come.

"So much trouble . . . and we haven't found the proof of Merlin's existence yet!" said Ravi, sighing. He threw a flat stone in the water and made it bump three times. He was hungry and sleepy, and he felt guilty for the trouble he had caused with the monkey. He also felt guilty about all his fears. There was nothing he could do about his phobias, but perhaps he could do something to save their adventure. "What if we go back into the animals' room and find the proof?"

Minerva and Thomasina looked at him, surprised.

"Really?" asked Thomasina. "I was sure you wouldn't want to go in there again."

Ravi got on his feet. "Well, I do! We can't let Tristam win this!"

Thomasina hugged him. "You're so brave, Ravi!" she yelled.

He blushed and said, "Come on, let's go. We don't have time to waste."

They went back inside the cave, and this time everything was easier. They followed the chalk numbers and found the room of animals without a problem. They looked at the creatures without daring to touch them for fear of another trap.

"Now what?" asked Thomasina.

They stood at the center of the cave, back to back, the flashlights pointed toward the animals.

Minerva frowned. The humidity had made her hair even curlier and fluffier.

"I know which one was Merlin's favorite animal," she said, stepping forward.

She bent in front of an owl and examined it.

Ravi and Thomasina were behind her.

"The owl represents wisdom," Minerva explained. "And Merlin was the wisest of all." She slowly stretched one arm toward the carving.

Without even realizing it, Ravi and Thomasina grabbed each other's hands for courage. Who knew what was going to happen now?

Minerva carefully touched the owl, but nothing happened. They all breathed in relief, and the tension went away.

Minerva handled him a bit more and the statue opened, revealing a hole. The girl leaned over to look. She put one hand inside and pulled out a book. She lit it with her flashlight. On the cover, there was some type of seal, with the image of a flower, a sword, and a cane.

"Let me see!" said Thomasina.

She was about to open the book, but Minerva stopped her. "No! It's very old. We might ruin it. We have to give it to Tristam. He'll know what to do."

They started back to shore. Minerva held the book tightly to her chest to protect it.

Outside, the sun was rising. The sea was still a dark bulk, but you could see a pink sparkle in the east.

A tiny rocky strip emerged from the water: their only connection with the mainland. It looked so fragile. Maybe their weight had damaged it the previous day.

Ravi gallantly said, "Let's go one at a time. Ladies first, Minerva."

Minerva crossed it with the book, and Thomasina followed her without problems. Ravi was last. He was the heaviest, and he felt the rock collapsing under his feet with every step he took. He stopped halfway, not sure whether to continue or go back.

Minerva and Thomasina tried to encourage him.

"Come on, you're going to make it!"

"Don't stop!"

Ravi moved one foot. Suddenly, the path started to crumble and the rock where Ravi stood sank. He fell in the water and tried to grab what was left of the natural bridge, but the currents were so strong that they dragged him away. He furiously moved his arms and legs to stay on the surface. But whenever he came close to grabbing on to something, he was pulled away. Minerva and Thomasina watched in terror.

"He might crash against the cliffs!" said Minerva.

"What are we going to do?" asked Thomasina. "Should we jump into the water?"

It didn't seem like the best solution: the current would probably drag them away as well.

Minerva recalled what Agatha had told her: *You'll know when it's the right time . . .*

She looked at Thomasina. "The little bag that Agatha gave us!" she yelled. "Do you still have it?

Her friend reached inside the purse and handed the bag over.

Minerva undid the blue ribbon. It was some type of firework shaped as a candle. On one side, it had a paper-like flap. She pulled it, and a bright light shot up into the sky with a whistle and opened up. If the situation had not been so desperate, Minerva would have been mesmerized.

When all the little flames went off, they heard a furious bark. Pendragon showed up on the beach

as fast as a missile. He plunged into the water and reached Ravi. In his panic, the boy was kicking like crazy. But when the dog got close enough, Ravi grabbed onto his long fur and let himself be dragged to the shore.

"Wow, that was another close one!" Ravi said, once he was safe on the beach.

Pendragon was happily licking his face, as if to reassure him that everything was all right. Ravi hugged him. "You're my hero, Pendragon!"

"Minerva!" someone yelled. "Thomasina! Ravi!"

Minerva looked around. "It's Agatha!" she said.

Pendragon started barking again. He recognized his owner as well.

Agatha hurried to them. When she saw that everyone was okay, she paused to catch her breath. "Thank God you are all safe!" she said. "I was looking for you. I was so worried." Agatha looked at Minerva. "Last night I went to your house, and the woman there told me that you still hadn't made it back. I figured you went to Tintagel, and then I saw the flare go off." She let herself fall on the beach. "Agh! I was so scared! I shouldn't have shown you the runes."

Minerva smiled. "Everything is just fine. We found proof that Merlin existed," she said, showing her the book. "And you saved us. What was that? Fireworks?"

Agatha was still catching her breath. "Kind of. It's called a flare. We use them in the heath moor whenever there's an accident. They're useful to indicate the position of someone who's gotten lost."

"Well, it worked," said Ravi, still holding onto Pendragon. He wasn't sure he'd ever let him go.

Suddenly, they heard footsteps. Someone else was coming. Tristam appeared in front of them. When he saw them, he stopped. But he wasn't looking at the three young friends. He was looking at Agatha.

He slowly walked closer to her. "You . . . you are . . ."

She smiled and her blue eyes slightly turned upward. "I'm Agatha."

Tristam was admiring her as if he could not believe she was real. "I saw you around Tintagel's ruins one morning . . . I thought you were a ghost."

"But you don't believe in ghosts!" Minerva reminded him.

"Yes, they're not scientific enough," said Ravi, giggling.

But Tristam didn't even hear them. He was completely mesmerized by the heath moor's witch!

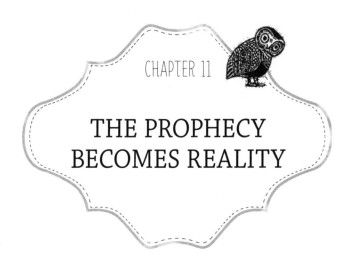

CHAPTER 11

THE PROPHECY BECOMES REALITY

Agatha seemed amused by Tristam's confusion. "I'm not a ghost. See?" she said, holding out her arms.

She looked so beautiful, glowing in the pink and blue lights reflected by the sea. All Tristam could do was babble. "I looked for you in town, but no one was like you," he said.

"I don't live in Pembrose," said Agatha. "I live in Bodmin Heath Moor."

"She's a witch," whispered Minerva with satisfaction.

Tristam put one hand in his hair. "A . . . what?"

"A witch," Thomasina repeated.

"I suppose you don't believe in witches either," said Minerva, poking fun at him.

Tristam sighed. "Well, if they're this beautiful . . ."

Agatha's cheeks were flushed, and she lowered her eyes, breaking the spell.

"Hey, Tristam, why are you here?" asked Ravi suddenly.

The archaeologist woke up from his daze and looked at the three friends. "I was checking one last thing at the castle ruins when I saw the flare. I thought someone was in danger."

"Someone *was* in danger . . . me! But Pendragon saved me," Ravi said.

The dog licked Ravi's face again to confirm that that's how it went. He was proudly wagging his tail, happy to be the center of attention.

Minerva walked over to Tristam and solemnly gave him the book. "This is for you, Mr. Archaeologist."

Tristam looked surprised. "What is it?" He took

the old volume and looked at the cover. He frowned. The Order of the Owls held their breath.

Tristam examined the seal and became pale. "Where did you find this?"

"Inside Merlin's cave," said Thomasina.

"The real one," added Minerva.

"We found it!" Ravi announced proudly.

Pendragon barked to confirm they were telling the truth.

Agatha felt like she had to explain her side of the story. She told Tristam about the runes carved on the rocks in the heath moor. And the others told him about their adventure inside the cave.

The archaeologist shook his head. "Unbelievable!" He looked at the seal again. "It looks real. The heather's flower represents the old Cornwall reign, the sword is Arthur's Excalibur, and the cane is Merlin's symbol. It means old age and wisdom."

The three friends looked at one another and grinned. It seemed they had succeeded.

Tristam carefully opened the volume and was

shocked. "I can't believe it!" he said. The friends were suddenly worried.

Tristam kept flipping through the pages, more and more excited. "They're Merlin's prophecies!" He looked at the three children with admiration. "You three have made an extraordinary discovery!"

Ravi, Minerva, and Thomasina straightened their backs, and their chests filled with pride. The Order of the Owls had done it again!

* * *

That same afternoon, Tristam publicly apologized to the entire village in front of the London journalists. He winked at the three friends, who were watching him from their favorite place on the dock, and announced that he had been wrong — Pembrose was, in fact, home to Merlin's authentic cave. The proof was a book of prophecies that he found in the cave under Tintagel Castle.

Before Tristam gave his speech, everyone decided together not to reveal the existence of the real cave. It would be kept a secret, just like Merlin wanted. And they wouldn't disclose Minerva, Ravi, and Thomasina's role in finding it. The Order of the Owls preferred to be anonymous, Minerva explained.

They told their parents and Mrs. Flopps that they had spent the night at Tristam's camp, because they had lost track of time while helping him with some research. The archaeologist apologized over and over. Everyone was so happy about the book that he was quickly forgiven, even by the stern Sir Archibald and Lady Annabella. Minerva contained her laughter by covering her mouth with her hands. She had to bear a terrible tickle to her feet, but it was for a good cause.

Tristam ended his speech with one of his charming smiles, saying, "The book with the great sorcerer's prophecies will remain in Pembrose. It will be a symbol of pride for the whole village!"

Everyone clapped their hands and, with a wave from the mayor, the village's band started to play the national anthem. Everyone stood up and sang. The villagers were very satisfied. The Sea Festival could continue, and many tourists would come to admire Merlin's famous book.

"Good thing he didn't take it to London with him," said Ms. Haddok.

"What a great day for our village!" Araminta Bartholomew said with a sigh. She seemed to devour the handsome archaeologist with her eyes.

"I wonder . . . are these prophecies even true?" asked an old fisherman who was ready to go out to sea.

"Who cares? As long as tourists believe in them," his mate replied, putting the nets on the boat.

But, yes, were Merlin's prophecies true? Before giving the book to Pembrose's mayor, Tristam walked toward the three friends. Agatha was with them as well. Her blue eyes sparkled with a smile.

Tristam opened the book. "This morning I took a look at the prophecies. And take a look here!"

The friends stretched their necks.

"I can't understand what it says."

"What language is that?"

"They're not runes . . ."

Tristam shook his head. "It's some type of secret code, a blend of Nordic, Celtic, and Latin languages that Merlin used so no one could understand him."

"One of Merlin's tricks," said Ravi, sighing.

Pendragon was there as well, and the boy kept scratching his head, to the dog's immense satisfaction.

"So, what does it say?" Minerva asked, impatient.

Tristam gave a look at Agatha. "Here it says that a young, long-blond-haired, stubborn stranger will fall in love with a local witch whose eyes are as blue as the sea . . ."

Minerva looked at him closely. Was he telling the truth? She felt a mild tickle under her feet, but maybe they were just tingling because she had been sitting down for so long. Who knew? After all, it was not that important. Tristam looked like he was in love with Agatha, and it was clear that the feeling was mutual.

The young archaeologist took the young witch's hand. "You three were right; not everything can be explained," he said. "Love, for example."

Agatha blushed. She was taken by surprise, but she didn't pull her hand away.

Minerva sighed. *Love is some kind of magic*, she thought. *A beautiful kind of magic.*

Ravi peeked at the book. What if there was some prophecy about him and Thomasina? Would he ever be able to conquer her heart? Too bad he couldn't read the book. He would just have to wait and see how things went.

CHAPTER 12

OWL
TOWER

Tourists started to arrive right after the book was found. They wandered the streets of Pembrose, taking pictures of everything from the nice cottages painted in white, to the bay among the cliffs, to the amazing turquoise-green sea.

Meanwhile, the members of the Order of the Owls were already bored. They spent their warm, lazy afternoons lying on the grass of Lizard Manor.

"Oh, I wish we had another mystery to solve!" said Thomasina. "I'm bored to death!"

"We've just had a ton of trouble!" Ravi reminded her. "A little bit of rest will do us good." But he didn't sound too convinced himself.

"We still have to find out what happened to Minerva's parents," Thomasina said.

"That won't be easy," said Ravi, suffocating a yawn. "There are so many clues in the travel bag. We'll need time."

They had just finished a heavy snack, a delicious date-and-walnut pie, from Mrs. Kapoor. All that remained were a few crumbs on the cloth.

Minerva lay on her back with a piece of grass in her mouth. She was studying the sky. The clouds looked like soft sheep. She could also see a tiny corner of the roof and Augustus, the big snowy owl, overlooking the highest chimney. He had his head lowered and his eyes half closed. But he was attentive; he immediately realized when someone was coming and opened his yellow eyes.

There was an excited bark and Pendragon crossed the grass in a rush to jump on top of Ravi.

"Hey!" yelled the boy, rolling in the grass while the dog tried to lick his face.

"Hi, lazies!" Agatha greeted them. "Do you feel like going on a little trip with me?"

All three of them stood right up, ready to go.

* * *

Agatha's Jeep shook on the narrow paths of the heath moor. The three friends were sitting in the backseat, anxious and excited.

"Where are we going?" asked Ravi.

"Is it an adventure?" asked Thomasina.

"Do you need our help?" added Minerva.

Agatha smiled in the rearview mirror. "It's a surprise," she said.

"But . . ." started Ravi.

"Enough with these questions!" said Agatha. "Wait and see. We're almost there."

They kept driving for a little longer, and the three of them had to contain their curiosity. On their left side, they saw a stretch of sea, interrupted here and there by the white foam of the waves. A soft, salty breeze blew through the windows and messed up Minerva's hair.

At last, the Jeep stopped and the three friends jumped out. They looked around, full of expectation.

"So? Can you tell us what the surprise is?" asked Thomasina.

"Why did you bring us here?" added Ravi.

It seemed like there was nothing interesting to see — just the sea on one side and the grass hills on the other.

"Shhh! You'll know in a bit. Follow me!" said Agatha.

They followed her down a rocky path. After a few minutes, they saw a stone building, a tower of some sort. It looked familiar, but they were still too far away to realize that they had seen it before.

Standing by the tower, someone was waving at them. Finally they could see it was Tristam.

Pendragon, happy to be out of the car, ran around like crazy, barking and wagging his tail.

When they were close enough, Minerva paused and looked at the tower. It had a curious shape. The bottom was rounded and it narrowed at the top like a vase.

Agatha smiled at her. "I thought this would be perfect for your hideout."

Minerva looked around. The place *was* perfect: it sat on top of a hill, facing the sea and the heath moor. The building looked old and solid.

"So, do you like it?" asked Tristam. "Are you surprised?"

"But . . . it's . . ." Minerva started. "It's identical to the tower that's on the box the flute was in!"

"Wow, you're right!" said Ravi.

"It's called Owl Tower," said Agatha. "It's been abandoned for many years. It seemed like the ideal hideout for the Order of the Owls to me."

Minerva looked up toward the battlements. Their hideout . . . the same tower carved on the box that now was on the nightstand at Lizard Manor. One of many mysteries to be unveiled.

Thomasina was very excited. "We finally have a hideout, a secret place all to ourselves!"

But it was time for more surprises. Tristam wore a sly smile, as if he was hiding something else. "Come with me!" he said, waving them along.

They followed him behind the tower. Leaning

against the wall were two brand-new bicycles. A red one and a pink one.

"Are they for us?" asked Minerva and Thomasina.

Tristam nodded. "Yes, to thank you for your help and . . . well, to apologize for all the trouble that I caused," he added, a little bit embarrassed. "I've been hideous, haven't I?"

Minerva smiled at him. "Terribly hideous!" she answered, laughing. "But you're getting better."

Agatha stepped closer to the young archaeologist and took his hand. "Now you can get to your hideout by bike — all three of you!" she said.

"And I won't have to give you a ride home from school anymore," said Ravi. Actually, he was a little disappointed that he wouldn't be giving Thomasina rides anymore. It always made him feel like he was a knight on horseback, helping a beautiful damsel.

Minerva immediately jumped on the seat of the red bicycle. Thomasina followed her lead and jumped on the pink one. They left in a hurry, followed by Pendragon, who tried to keep up, barking loudly.

"Hurray, the Order of the Owls solved another mystery!" shouted Minerva, pedaling her feet.

"And we found a hideout!" yelled Thomasina, dangerously cutting in front of Minerva.

Ravi covered his eyes with his hand. He couldn't bear to watch. Those two were sure to get into trouble!

Elisa at age 3

As a child, I had red hair. It was so red that it led to several nicknames, the prettiest of which was Carrot. With my red hair, I wanted to be Pippi Longstocking for two reasons. The first reason was that I wanted to have the strength to lift a horse and show him to everyone! The second was that every night my mother read Astrid Lindgren's books to me until she nearly lost her voice (or until I graciously allowed her to go to bed). As I fell asleep each night, I hoped to wake up at Villa Villacolle. Instead, I found myself in Milan. What a great disappointment!

After all of Lindgren's books were read and reread, my mother, with the excuse that I was grown up, refused to continue to read them again. So I began to tell stories myself. They were serialized stories, each more and more intricate than the one before and chock-full of interesting characters. Pity then, the next morning, when I would always forget everything.

Elisa today

At that point I had no choice; I started to read myself. I still remember the book that I chose: a giant-sized edition of the Brothers Grimm fairy tales with a blue cloth cover.

Today my hair is less red, but reading is still my favorite pastime. Pity it is not a profession because it would be perfect for me!

GABO LEON BERNSTEIN

I was born in Buenos Aires, Argentina, and have had to overcome many obstacles to become an illustrator.

"You cannot draw there," my mom said to me, pointing to the wall that was smeared.

"You cannot draw there," the teacher said to me, pointing to the school book that was messed.

"Draw where you want to . . . but you were supposed to hand over the pictures last week," my publishers say to me, pointing to the calendar.

Currently I illustrate children's books, and I'm interested in video games and animation projects. The more I try to learn to play the violin, the more I am convinced that illustrating is my life and my passion. My cat and the neighbors rejoice in it.

Gabo

WHAT'S NEXT FOR
THE ORDER OF THE OWLS?

ELISA PURICELLI GUERRA

THE LEGEND OF
BLACK BART

The mystery of Minerva's parents is pushed aside once again when the ghost of old Black Bart, a cruel pirate, wreaks havoc in the village of Pembrose. Legend has it that the old pirate was so mean during his life that his spirit cannot find peace until he performs a good deed. Minerva is certain that she can convince Bart to do just that, but first she and her friends have to find him. Will the search for Black Bart's spirit lead Minerva and her friends into danger?

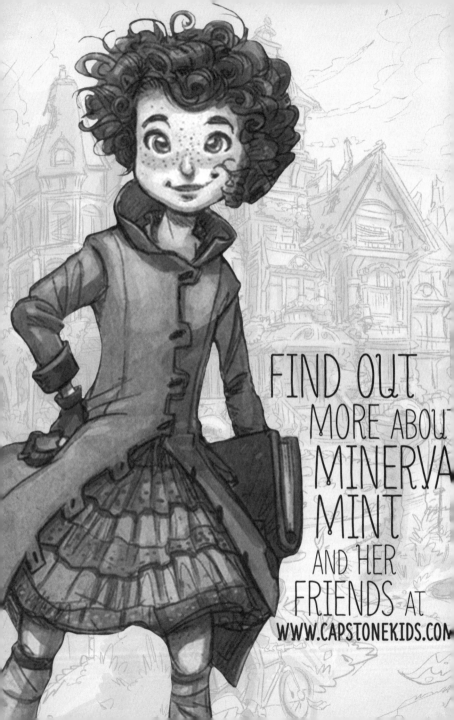

FIND OUT
MORE ABOUT
MINERVA
MINT
AND HER
FRIENDS AT
WWW.CAPSTONEKIDS.COM